T0367867

Seeking a Better Life

Inspired by True Stories

EDWARD SETO

WESTBOW®
PRESS
A DIVISION OF THOMAS NELSON
& ZONDERVAN

WestBow Press books may be ordered through booksellers or by contacting:

WestBow Press
A Division of Thomas Nelson & Zondervan
1663 Liberty Drive
Bloomington, IN 47403
www.westbowpress.com
1 (866) 928-1240

ISBN: 978-1-4908-2469-7 (sc)
ISBN: 978-1-4908-2470-3 (hc)
ISBN: 978-1-4908-2468-0 (e)

Library of Congress Control Number: 2014901843

Printed in the United States of America.

WestBow Press rev. date: 03/03/2014

To my parents and grandparents.
To my uncles, aunts, and cousins.
To my sister and my nephew.
To my wife, children, and grandchildren with love.

When Eric was a small boy, he dreamed of one day writing a story for his grandparents, Arakssi and Agop.

He did not know exactly why, but he wanted to do something for them to preserve images and remember the stories of their lives.

Not that they were extraordinary people, but they were the ones he loved. Sometimes he felt sad for the difficulties they had endured; sometimes he admired them and sometimes he was not very proud of them, but he always loved them.

Then his life moved forward faster than he expected, and he turned into a grown man.

He had been married to Renee for more than thirty years, and they had two beautiful, grown daughters, Nevena and Maya. The family immigrated to Canada about twenty years ago.

Still, from time to time, he remembered the young Eric talking to his grandfather, Mezhairig Agop, and grandmother, Mezmama Arakssi, saying, "I will one day write a story of your lives."

Now in his mid-fifties, he still says that when he retires, he will write a story for his family, as simple as they were and as boring as a story of ordinary people can be.

He doesn't know if he will finish it, but if he doesn't start, there will certainly be no book and no stories, and he would then be a liar to his relatives.

Eric started to talk to himself while seated at his desk at home. "I hate to lie, even though sometimes when I'm challenged by people, I say exaggerated things; afterward, I hate it. I guess this is how things have worked for me, and I get things done. I have a big mouth, and then I have to do it.

"Our kids, Nevena and Maya, while they were still small, quickly learned the trick to make me say things, and then they'd say, 'You promised me ...' So, I had to do it.

"Of course, this was one of the ways they got me to do things. Plus there was always the line of responsibility, the things I had to do to make the people I love happy.

"I want to see my family happy. So I'm busy, and most of the time, I'm happy.

"Let's get into writing this story and see what will come out of all this."

July 2008

Renee and Eric went on a two-week vacation to Bulgaria and Greece, and they had a good time.

They spent a week in Greece with Lisa and Arak, his sister and her husband, and then they went together to Balchik on the Black Sea coast of Bulgaria for four days. He was able to improve his sister's mood and change her daily routine.

Lisa and Arak had taken very good care of his mother, Nelly. Eric felt very bad that he couldn't spend enough time with his mother. He saw her once a year, when he took vacations to Bulgaria. He and his wife would stay for about a week with her and then go to their apartment on the Black Sea coast. On the way back, he would see his mother again for a few more days before taking the plane to Ottawa.

Last December, Nelly passed away just a day before her seventy-fifth birthday. It was unexpected, even though she had not been doing well for more than a year. Eric spoke with her on the phone the day before she left this world. He took a plane and was there for the funeral, spending a week with Lisa. She was not in good shape—she was emotionally exhausted and physically tired. She certainly had not told him how difficult the last five months had been since Eric saw his mother for the last time. He promised his sister to take them on vacation to Greece next summer. Lisa and Arak were both retired, so they were always careful how to spend their small pensions.

When Eric and Renee came to Bulgaria, he brought them a brand-new laptop so they could keep in touch on Skype. Using the Internet was a relatively new way to see each other. Too bad he couldn't do that when his mother was still alive. His sister was initially afraid that she could not manage the new laptop, but soon she learned how to open Skype and how to speak and see Eric on it. She and Arak learned quickly how to check their e-mails and to browse the Internet. This was going to keep them busy.

In Greece, they stayed for a week at an all-inclusive resort on the coast of Khalkidhiki. Eric rented a van for a day, and they took a tour around the Cassandra Peninsula. The weather was good, and the beauty of the Greek peninsula made them dream of coming here again. They celebrated Lisa's birthday on the balcony of the resort restaurant, with rich food, bottles of champagne and wonderful views.

When they came back to Bulgaria, they stayed for a day in Lisa's home, and the next day, they went to Balchik. Here they met with Eric and Lisa's cousin,

Alexa, and her husband, Dinko. Eric was happy to spend time with his cousin's family. Unfortunately, their son, Boris, was not with them in Balchik. He was busy working in Sofia.

Boris was part of the new generation of young, successful businessmen in Bulgaria. He had graduated from the American Business University in Bulgaria and later, together with three other friends from the same university, started a software company in 2002. Soon, their company became a preferred supplier for Microsoft in Eastern Europe.

Dinko was working as a representative of an American company, selling machines to factories in Eastern Europe, the Middle East, and Africa.

Dinko and Boris had bought two apartments just in front of the marina. The bigger apartment was for Alexa and Dinko, and the other one was for Boris and his wife, Christy. They both had very good views of the sea.

Eric and Renee slept in Boris's apartment, overlooking the marina, the sea, and the whole Bay of Balchik. Lisa and Arak stayed in Alexa and Dinko's apartment. They all gathered together in the morning for coffee on Alexa and Dinko's balcony facing the swimming pool; right behind it was the sea. The view was gorgeous. The sun was just coming up, as if from the depths of the water.

They drank coffee, joked, and laughed. Eric sat there smiling, listening to the conversation. They made plans for the next few days before going back to Canada.

Though he was participating in the conversation, at the same time, Eric had not stopped thinking about their past and the time when they were kids.

He wanted to start writing this book about their grandparents. The idea of how to write it was slowly coming into his head, but still he was not ready.

He first needed to remember more about his childhood, and sitting next to his cousin, Alexa, was somehow helping him visualize it.

Eric started thinking, no longer following their conversation.

✍

Alexa hasn't changed much, and it really is a pleasure to be with them. They know how to enjoy life and good company.

Alexa likes talking about our childhood and Mezmama. I believe Mezmama is her favorite memory. She speaks about her with a lot of love. Recently, I found a picture of my grandmother and grandfather as a bride and groom. Mezmama Arakssi and Alexa are so much alike.

I haven't seen Alexa for years, and then, even when I saw her, it was just for a few hours or a day. It is strange, because as kids, we grew up together until about ten years of age. We lived in my father's house with our grandparents and my uncle Ed and his wife, Nadia. It was a big family—my grandparents, Agop and Arakssi; my mother, Nelly, and father, Santo; my sister, Lisa; and my uncle Ed, Aunty Nadia, and Alexa.

When I look at my cousin, I see our childhood, but there are not too many things I remember. Maybe it will come to me later. I know it's all there somewhere.

Somehow, my sister and Alexa remember well the bad things I did to them. I suppose I was not a quiet boy, and maybe I gave them a kick or a fist from time to time, as they recall. Strange—I don't remember it.

I remember well when we went to kindergarten, Alexa and I. There were two bigger twin brothers, and they kept pushing all the kids, till one day I hit one of them in the face. It must have been very hard, because I remember his mouth was bloodied and the teacher showed it to me, shouting and twisting my ears. I stayed there alone, scared, and punished in a small, dark room.

Alexa was crying and waiting for me outside until my grandmother came to take us home.

Our grandmother. Her name was Arakssi, but we all called her Mezmama. How she loved us. Oh, God! We were the most important things in her life—the grandchildren: Lisa, Eric, Alexa, Victoria, and Magdalena.

Victoria and Magdalena are the children of my father's sister, Vera, and Uncle Manuk.

They were at home every Sunday. Somebody at home cooked for the big family, and we were all there together. I did not have to count; I knew we were thirteen people as one big family. At that time, I didn't pay attention to who was doing what; we didn't have to do anything—just play in the backyard. One day my cousin Alexa and my uncle Ed and aunt Nadia moved to a new apartment. Still, though, almost every weekend our families got together.

That was the time we learned the stories about Mezhairig Agop and Mezmama Arakssi. It was like reading stories from books. The stories were scary and sad, but I felt proud that my grandparents made it through and now here we were all seated around them on Sundays.

My grandparents and my parents worked all day long, even on Saturdays. My father and my mom left as early as 5:30 a.m. in the mornings to go to the shoe factory. Mezmama cooked. Whenever Mezhairig did not feel sick, he spread glue on the leather shoe parts or turned the edges nicely with a hammer and then sewed them on a Singer machine. I learned to do all of the parts of making shoes, just as a game. Nobody asked me to work as they did.

My mom and father came home from work at 4:00 p.m. After a short rest, they were working again, finishing Mezhairig and Mezmama's work. I don't recall anybody ever complaining that we had a hard life. Maybe life was easy? For sure, it was easy for us kids.

When I was a kid about seven or eight years old, I kept asking my grandfather to tell me the stories again. Then I asked my grandmother to tell me her stories again. They both did—over and over, until I learned them by heart.

My grandfather was born in Adapazar, a small town or village about 130 kilometers southeast of Istanbul in Turkey. He loved his town and his country. There were many Armenians living in Adapazar. According to my grandfather, about twenty thousand Armenians left Adapazar, never to go back again. Some of them survived; some of them didn't. This was from 1915 to 1921, when Armenians in Adapazar were either killed or left to die in deserts or sent to the war front to fight against England or Greece.

Armenian children and parents had to leave their homes, forced out by the Turkish rulers, and had to cross on foot the entire country, escorted by soldiers. Most of them died. Some were able to survive and got to Syria. During these long years, many Armenian boys and girls were stolen and forcefully sold into Kurdish, Arab, or Turkish families. A few years later, the world discovered the tragedy of the Armenian genocide.

My grandfather was one of the survivors. He was twenty-two or twenty-three years old in 1921 when he was taken into the army as a soldier. For three months, he was in a training camp on the outskirts of Istanbul.

One night a friend of his—a Turkish soldier—told him that on the next day, he would be chosen to go to the front. His friend had found out that all the Armenians would be sent to very difficult areas on the Greek front and were not expected to come back alive.

❧

"Hey, wake up!" Renee said to Eric. "Are you here? What are you thinking about?" She looked at him with an expression that said, "Hey, you are not alone here."

"We've been talking for an hour, and you have not said a word." Alexa pushed her cousin as they used to do when they were kids.

"I'm okay. I'm sorry. I'm just flooded with memories about our grandparents and our childhood," Eric said. "I know that's strange when we are sitting on the balcony and enjoying the summer and the sea."

He went on, "You know, I decided to write a book about our grandparents and how they came to Bulgaria a hundred years ago running for their lives."

He was shy and felt uncomfortable telling them that he was planning to write a book. It sounded like such a big task, and he wasn't sure that he could do it.

"I'm sorry. I know it is not the time now to talk about these things, so please allow me to just be silent for a while."

Alexa was excited, and she did not let him change the subject until he finally told them a little about his idea. He started telling them about his memories of their childhood and the story of his grandfather, Agop.

"So what happened when Agop understood that he would be sent to the most difficult places on the front?" Alexa asked.

Eric continued the story.

❧

That night Mezhairig had to make a decision between going to the front and probably dying there, or perhaps dying while he was trying to escape.

The next morning, all the soldiers were taken out for shooting practice.

When his turn came, Agop picked up the rifle and aimed at a stone next to the target. He was hoping that if he didn't hit the target, they would leave him in the camp for some more training. He pulled the trigger, and the stone exploded.

The sergeant tapped on his shoulder and said, "*Aferim!* [Bravo!] Soldier, you are ready to fight for your country."

That same day he was put with all the other young soldiers on the train leaving Istanbul.

Istanbul was a big cosmopolitan city. The capital of Turkey, it was full of reporters and embassies. All the advanced culture of Turkey was concentrated there. Most of the progressives Turks were living in Istanbul.

The train slowly departed, and with every kilometer, Agop's hopes of escaping decreased.

Agop told his sergeant that he needed to go to the bathroom, and the sergeant walked him to the door. Once inside, he locked the door and braced the rifle behind it. He opened the window. It was scary and his heart beat rapidly, but he well knew that this was his only chance. Without hesitating anymore, he jumped out the window.

Thankfully, he did not have anything broken, and no one had seen him jump out. He stood up and quickly ran away from the train tracks and into the forest to wait for the sun to go down and the moon to rise.

Agop had to walk several days back to Istanbul, always without letting anyone notice him. Nobody stopped him. He slept during the days and walked during the nights. Four days later, early in the morning, he entered the big city. He went straight to his relatives. Agop had not been able to contact his family since he'd been drafted three months earlier. There he found out that his mother, with his older brother, sister, and her husband had managed to leave Istanbul; they were now in Plovdiv, Bulgaria.

During the Balkan War from October 1912 till May 1913, Bulgaria was fighting against Turkey for full independence. During the First World War from 1914 to 1918, however, Bulgaria was on the side of Germany and so was Turkey, so the border was relatively open and there was some communication between the two countries even though it was limited. Agop started to plan how to get to Bulgaria.

In the seaport, there were often boats going to Bulgaria, but to get on one of them, Agop needed money and papers. His relatives helped him to get a document showing that he was seventeen years old (too young for the draft) and with a false Turkish name. At that time, there were no pictures on personal documents, so he was able to walk around Istanbul and look for a job.

A few weeks later, he started working as a conductor on a tramway. A captain of a Bulgarian boat had promised to take him to Bulgaria for a certain amount of money, and now he had to work and save money as quickly as possible.

A month later, he was almost ready with the money—but in the train where he was working as a conductor, he noticed the same sergeant from the army. Agop turned his back to the sergeant, praying that he would not come to ask for a ticket. Luckily the man did not approach him to buy a ticket, and at the first stop, Agop left the train and went directly to the port to look for the boat and its captain.

The boat was in port. It was going to leave for Burgas in a few days, but Agop did not want to stay even one more day in the city. The captain took him on as a helper in the kitchen and allowed him to stay onboard the boat until they were underway.

A few days later, he was in Burgas on the Bulgarian sea coast, about 300 kilometers east of Plovdiv, with no money and nowhere to go. The only languages he knew were Armenian and Turkish.

How could he ask for directions? Who could he ask for help? He was scared. He was cold. He had a fever. He was afraid to talk to uniformed people because he was afraid they would send him back. This was his nightmare. He did not trust anybody. Slowly he made his way out of the port and into the city of Burgas.

It was raining, and it was late October. The leaves were almost gone from the trees, and the streets and the houses looked empty and cold. His heart was empty and his stomach was burning, but he felt sweaty and cold.

"How will I find my family?" he asked himself. "Where are they?"

He was walking the streets looking for something—he did not know what. Maybe he was looking for a miracle. He was young.

He was alone in this foreign world. Finally he picked up the smell of freshly made bread, and he just headed for it like a hungry dog. The smell was coming from an old bakery. There were people waiting outside—hungry people like him. Some of them looked very poor and beaten from life. They were all waiting for somebody to give them a piece of bread. It was wartime, and many people were hungry.

Agop joined the queue with these people. They all looked like him—tired and wearing old clothes. He felt a bit better. He was not alone anymore. He felt even better when he heard some people talking Turkish.

These were gypsies. He told them that he was Armenian and was looking for an Armenian church or some other place where he could meet with other Armenians.

He was lucky again. A few hours later, he was in the Armenian church, where hundreds of other Armenians were gathered. These were survivors who came out of Turkey one way or another. They all had their stories.

❧

At this point Eric stopped. He looked around a bit uncomfortably.

Everybody was listening attentively, and they were expecting him to continue.

Eric didn't know how to go on with his story. He coughed, smiled, and said, "Writing a story about somebody's life could be done really fast, but how do I write about what his feelings were, what made him happy, what made him afraid, what made him and the others keep on going when it was very difficult? So many strong feelings! I'm trying to imagine them, but it is not working well."

Alexa jumped from her seat and hugged him. "I'm sure you will find a way to do it. It is very good. Please do not stop; continue working on this book."

They all encouraged him to write, and they said that they would be waiting with interest to see how he would develop the stories and how he would write about their own emigration to Canada.

Eric was not feeling comfortable with their expectations.

"This is a difficult task. I'm not sure how I'm going to do it. I need to come to Bulgaria again and talk to my aunt Vera and uncle Ed and find out more details about our grandparents.

"But in few days, we are going home to Ottawa. I have to go to work and wait till next summer. Unfortunately, when I start working, I have no time to think about anything else. So I will have to put it on hold.

"Maybe next year we will be able to come again on vacation. Here in Bulgaria, I will have the time. I hope to hear new stories, and maybe my uncle and my aunt will remember more about the lives of their parents. I hope I will remember more myself."

They spoke a bit more about the book and their childhood, and soon after that, they went back into discussing the summer activities for the next few days.

The weather was fantastic. The mood of everybody was good, and they all went out to enjoy the rest of their vacation.

Summer 2010

Two years passed, and Eric had not written anything. He was busy with his work at Seda Inc. and the problems he had with his second cousin and business partner, Dave.

Eric and Renee went to Bulgaria again for their summer vacation. They had an apartment at Sunny Beach, which they bought in 2003. It was a one-bedroom apartment in a well-kept resort development about 250 meters from the beach in the foothills of the mountain. It was a wonderful location, with a perfect climate. Nearby was a sanatorium for kids with asthma and bronchitis. There always was a breeze from the mountain and from the sea, so the air was fresh and full of oxygen.

The place was a bit noisy, because a street was below, not far from their balcony. They hoped that the municipality of the nearby city of Nessebar would build a new road around the new limits of the resort to stop the traffic. Sunny Beach is the main beach resort of Bulgaria, and hundreds of thousands of tourists visit it every summer.

Eric went with his wife to the beach every day. He sat under the umbrella among hundreds of people, watching the sea and practically not seeing or hearing anything. Renee knew his problems, and she let him try to sort them out in his head. She was patient and understanding.

How lucky I am to have Renee for my wife and mother of our children! Eric thought. He looked at her and right away felt much better.

When they got married in 1978, he took her to a hotel in Sunny Beach. At the time, everything there was the property of the government. He had promised her that one day they would have their own apartment right in the heart of the resort. It was one more promise he kept.

In the summer of 2003 during their vacation, they were going from Varna to Sunny Beach, crossing the Balkan Mountain with his sister, Lisa, and her husband, Arak. On the last turn of the road before starting to descend, a gorgeous view of the Black Sea and the bay of Sunny Beach appeared. Arak pulled the car over so they could see the new developments better. Eric and Renee couldn't believe their eyes. The resort had doubled in size. Everywhere for 250 meters from the coastline were new construction and new beautiful hotels and vacation villages. Just below the mountain was a new vacation village, facing the beach.

Three hours later, Eric had bought an apartment there. He was happy to see his wife smiling.

Now Sunny Beach was even larger, with brand-new hotels and blocks of apartments with owners from all over the world. Bulgaria is now part of the European Union, and many ordinary people from Europe bought inexpensive, but beautiful, apartments.

Eric brought his thoughts back to his work and his business partner. He had to make a decision about his future, or better said their future.

"What are you thinking about?" Renee looked at him with a sense of wariness. "You need to relax. Take it easy. You are tired, and you need a change. Let's go in the water. It's getting too hot here."

"No, no, you go. I will stay here under the umbrella. I need to remember everything we went through, and I have to find my balance again. I have to be sure I'm not going to make a mistake. I have to make a decision."

"Do you want to talk with me? It is important for you to know what my opinion is, isn't it?" Renee asked.

"Yes, but I'm not ready yet. I need some time to really sort out all the events in my head, trying not to get emotional. I need to stay cool. If I get upset, the decision will be quick, but may be wrong. We will talk later, maybe tomorrow."

"Okay, but the sooner, the better. This is taking too long, and I see you are torturing yourself. You cannot sleep normally, we barely talk …"

"Okay, I promise we will discuss it in detail. The decision will be ours, not just mine."

Eric was overwhelmed with thoughts about what was happening at Seda Inc. and his partnership with Dave, which seemed to be coming to an end. As soon as he got back from vacation, Eric was supposed to give Dave his final decision whether he was going to leave or stay.

It is not easy to separate from a partner in a business after you have spent almost twenty years working together, Eric was thinking.

Memories started coming back to him.

❧

In early 1990 after the fall of the communist regime in Bulgaria, many people started leaving the country. It was becoming unbearable to stay in Bulgaria. The economy collapsed. There were long lines in every store for everything, and the value of money had fallen sharply. Thousands of young people went to Western Europe, Canada, or the United States and stayed there as refugees, hoping to have a better future for them and their children.

At that time, he made a decision to leave Bulgaria and start working for a company in Western Europe or Canada. He spoke with his wife, and she supported him 100 percent. She was ready to follow him to any place in the world where they could make their home, as long it was better than Bulgaria. Their children would blame them for the decision.

Eric started outlining his thoughts silently in his head as if he were talking to somebody else. This was a powerful way for him to remember what had happened:

I did not want to leave the country as a refugee. I was sending my CV to companies in Germany and England with which I had some connection from before, when I was working in the automation laboratory and later at Biotech Bulgaria.

I also wrote a letter to my uncle Avedis in Ottawa, Canada, who owned a factory that was producing furniture components.

It was a very dry letter, and I did not have much hope of anything coming from it. Basically I was saying here is my CV. Here are copies of some of my achievements—diploma of the university in Plovdiv from which I graduated with excellence, additional one-month training in London, two gold medals on a national Bulgarian level as a young (up to thirty years old) leader of young teams in product development. I had five years' experience as a leader of a product-development department in a specialized automation laboratory. I had five more years of experience as a leader of the product-development department at Biotech Bulgaria.

Then I wrote that I was looking for a job and I was ready to move right away with my family if there was an opportunity. I told him also that my father didn't know that I was writing this letter, so if he found that my services were not needed, he could refuse me without feeling bad.

And that was it. There was no sentence of "Please help me" or "Life is so difficult here in Bulgaria." This could have been a letter to somebody not related to my family, and maybe I felt a little bit better this way.

I had seen Uncle Avedis only once, when I was a kid of thirteen years old. At this time, he was already living in Canada; he was the rich and proud Uncle Avedis visiting his poor relatives in communist Bulgaria. I remember at the time, I was arguing with him and defending my country against his criticism, so on the next day, he brought me a present of a red shirt to suit my philosophy. He tried to kiss me on the cheek, but I did not let him.

Uncle Avedis is a first cousin of my father, Santo, and my uncle Ed. It was actually my uncle Ed who Avedis called for information and references.

Edwin was the same age as Avedis, and they were friends. My uncle Ed was VP of a big Bulgarian corporation, so his opinion was very important for Avedis.

I had not said anything to my father or my uncle Ed; I did not have too much hope about Uncle Avedis giving me a job.

I'm sure Uncle Ed gave Avedis very good references about me, and so did my other uncle, Sarkis. Sarkis is also a first cousin to my father, Santo, and of course, to Avedis and Edwin. Sarkis and his wife, Antonia, lived in Bulgaria in the same city as we did. They were visiting Avedis and Armine in their big apartment on the twentieth floor overlooking downtown Ottawa. This was their first visit of a Western country, which only became possible after the fall of communism.

Life is full of surprises. I did not know that they were visiting when Avedis opened my letter. His first reaction was bad. Avedis was furious, wanting to know how I could write him such a letter and how I could expect him to help all his relatives in Bulgaria. Why should he do anything for any one of us? Then he passed the letter to Sarkis to read it.

Sarkis read the letter and calmly told Avedis that he had not seen anywhere in the letter a word of *please help me*. The only thing he saw was a CV and an opportunity for both sides to come to an agreement and job contract. Then Sarkis told him that if he were in Avedis's shoes, he wouldn't miss this opportunity. Avedis was looking for a production manager. He needed somebody he could trust, somebody capable who would not be afraid to work very hard. At the same time Eric and Renee were looking to immigrate to Canada. Eric was trying to find a job in a free, democratic country.

Soon after that, Avedis contacted me and offered me a job as a production manager in his factory.

It was a big surprise. We were very happy for this opportunity to go to Canada with a job contract. Now we had to talk to my parents and Renee's parents. This was tough.

They understood and accepted that was better to go to Canada. Renee's parents, Nikola and Nina, said that they were comfortable because we were going to Ottawa and I was going to work for a relative—a first cousin of Santo. My father just said okay, "Go; I understand," and he turned his head so I could not see the tears in his eyes. My mother was crying, but she also accepted it as a better decision than staying in Bulgaria.

❧

Eric again heard her voice full of pain and hope.

"Maybe sometime in the future, you can come back," she said.

Eric's eyes were red. He remembered his mother, Nelly. Then he continued to follow the string of his memories.

❧

We had time before receiving the visas. Avedis hired a lawyer to proceed with preparation of our documents.

In the meantime, Sarkis and Antonia came back to Plovdiv from their trip to Ottawa. They were both unhappy and morally beaten. I never got the details of what exactly happened, but they said they were humiliated. I think their humiliation was mostly due to the fact that they discovered a new world and realized what they had missed. They felt so ignorant next to Avedis and Armine in their colorful world, with so many wonderful things Sarkis and Antonia never dreamed of. Sarkis and Antonia discovered how much they had lost by not living a life of dreams and hopes and opportunities, as their relatives did in a free country. But this was not a matter of choice since they were citizens of a communist country; it was not their fault.

One day Sarkis called my father and told him that he would visit him in a few days and would like me to be there as well. We met at my parents' house, and both Sarkis and Antonia tried hard to assure my parents that this was a good decision and an excellent opportunity for us to get out of Bulgaria and build a new life in a free and wonderful country, Canada.

At the end when I was left alone with Sarkis, he told me, "Eric, it is not going to be easy for you and Renee. Working for Avedis is very difficult. Even his son is having a hard time with him. My advice to you is to stay close to Dave. He is a good guy and very capable. He has a heart and you will be able to work with him, but I do not think you can survive long with Avedis as your boss."

I looked at him, and I asked him, "Can you be more specific? What do you mean it will be very hard for me to work for Uncle Avedis?"

"It doesn't matter." Sarkis took a deep breath while looking at me with intensity in his eyes. I felt he wanted to say more, but he managed to hold himself back.

"Just remember what I told you and be patient." His voice showed that he was upset. Then slowly he relaxed and tried to smile. He put his hand on my shoulder and said, "You will be okay. I'm sure you will succeed. Work hard! At least you will have many more chances than I and your father had in this communist country …"

He stopped for a while. Then he looked down at his hands and continued, "We worked so hard, and what did we achieve? Nothing—only broken spirits and dashed hopes. You go, and you do it for your father. He will be proud of you!" He stood up slowly and wished me good luck.

This was the last time I saw him. A few months later, he passed away in his car driving back from Serbia, where he went to sell goods. Despite his bad health, he decided to push his luck and take a last chance to do some free trade after the fall of the wall. He made as much money in just a week as he did in a year under the communist rules.

He had a minor heart attack, but he would not ask for a help in a foreign country; he was sure somebody would take his money in the hospital. He pushed on, driving till he crossed the Bulgarian border. Just before going to the hospital in Sofia, he called his cousin Edwin. Despite the strong pain in his chest, he waited for Edwin in the car and gave him all the money he had made.

Uncle Ed told me that Sarkis was happy; he proved he was capable of succeeding. If he'd only had the chance to live long enough in a free country, he would have been very successful; he could have had a factory like Avedis. Unfortunately, he did not have this chance—the same as many others, my father included.

My father was sick, but he was hiding it from us. In my entire life, I never heard him complain about his health or about what he had to do. He was a strong man, and he did not want to discuss his pains with anybody. Even I did not know how serious his health condition was.

He went to the hospital for a few days—"just to do some tests," he said, and I believed him. I went to see him and found him in the hallway. Instead of talking about him and asking him how he was doing, I was thinking about my trip. I showed him a copy of the Ottawa newspaper *Citizen*, with an article and picture of Avedis. Avedis was writing something about the free-trade rules of NAFTA between Canada and the United States. I was excited to show the article to my father, but the only thing I got from him as a reaction was an unhappy face and a short statement: "Okay; go to him."

He turned and went to his room, and I was left in the corridor alone. After a short hesitation, I left the hospital.

Only now do I know he was really sick and he did not want to show it to me. I wonder what I would have done if I had known. I still would have taken my family to Canada, but at least I would have given my father a big hug and told him how much I loved him and how much I would miss him. Would I really have done that?

One thing I learned much later in my life in Canada was that somehow the old system in Bulgaria had taught us not to show our feelings; we did not know how to express them openly. It's shameful ... and it's sad.

The time came for us to go to the airport in Sofia. All our relatives were there in front of the house waiting for my father and mother to say good-bye to us. They were both sick and were barely able to walk. My father was trying very hard to hold back his tears, and my mother was crying while they were kissing their grandchildren. Then everybody climbed silently into the cars, and we drove in three cars to the airport.

It was the last time I saw my father alive, and now I blame myself for trying to be a macho and not showing him my feelings ...

In May 1991, we arrived in Ottawa. I started working for the company on the third day after we arrived.

Uncle Avedis opened his house to us, and we stayed with him and Aunt Armine for the first two weeks. I started looking for a furnished apartment as a temporary place to stay till we found a good apartment with an acceptable rent and signed a contract for a year. With

Dave's help, we rented an apartment on a monthly basis, and we moved out.

Avedis was very good toward my family, but at the same time, he was extremely demanding at work toward both me and his son, Dave.

Soon I noticed that Dave was disappointed. He was very capable, but his father would not listen enough to his advises and would not let him take the control of the company.

Dave was at the time vice president of manufacturing and marketing for his father's company.

Avedis was a powerful man, with a fine line of arrogance. It was tough working for him.

I remember in the first week of my work when he came downstairs in the factory, he came to me, kissed me in front of everybody, and then asked me, "How are you doing?"

When I started literally answering his question, he stopped me and said, "Listen, Eric, here we work, we do not talk. We will talk about that at home."

"Okay, I didn't know," I managed to say in confusion.

"Yes, you don't know many things in this country, and you'd better start forgetting everything you learned in your country because it was wrong." Then he turned quickly and left.

I had a work permit for three years that Avedis had received. He showed it to me and locked it in his drawer. I felt like a hostage.

As soon as we arrived in Ottawa, we started the process of becoming Canadian citizens.

My wife is very good at filling out official applications, so she went to the emigration office downtown and started the process.

We were accepted as permanent residents in just eight months by the Canadian Consulate in Boston, where we sent the application forms.

It was a happy day when we received the approved documents; we had to leave the country and enter again the same day as Canadian permanent residents.

Dave took us in his van, and we crossed the border to the United States and right away turned back, now with the proper stamps of the Canadian Emigration Office at the border.

We became Canadians and received Canadian passports in three years.

In early 1994 during a big recession in Canada and the United States, Avedis's company went bankrupt. Avedis was tired and sick. He lost everything. He was not able to start over again.

Dave made a bold decision to start a new company as soon as possible so we would not lose our customers. Dave offered me a partnership in the new company and the position of vice president of manufacturing and product development. Avedis gave his blessings to his son and supported morally his decisions. Dave took a second mortgage from the bank against his house and the new company, Seda Inc. He bought the machines back during a public auction. I had no money at the time and no house to take a second mortgage against, but as Dave said, my participation and assets in the company were my experience, knowledge, and dedication.

A very important part of the creation of Seda Inc. was the speed of transformation and the fact that the same key people were in charge. We kept ten of our key employees and provided the same items and services.

Dave showed me a few places he was considering to locate our factory. I went with him to all the locations our real estate agent suggested, and we checked them carefully. We had to make our decision in a matter of hours. We discussed the choices for a while, and finally chose one. The place was strategically close to a highway and not far from the airport. This was the most expensive compared to the other options, but we both agreed it was the right choice.

Dave convinced the owners of the building to give us a three-year lease with very good conditions for us. It was Thursday night, and he said the factory would start work at the new location on Monday morning at 7:00 a.m. This was such a bold approach that the old Jewish man who was the owner looked at us with admiration and shook our hands as a confirmation of a contract. We moved all the big presses, one double-head CNC (computer numeric control milling machines), and other small machines and tools and all the materials and product in process in just three days—over a weekend. This was amazing. Everything was planned in advance, and the moving company performed as per our notes. Some of the people and machines were still working at the old place, producing important customer orders, while other machines were moved and placed exactly on their well-marked spots on the floor. The electrical work and the plumbing and air-compression system were being installed by different crews, while the big presses and pallets with materials and pallets with products in process were moved to their places by the moving company. By Sunday midnight, we were done.

On Monday morning, all the employees came to the new place at 7:00 a.m. and started work as a normal working day. A new factory was born, and the place was beaming with energy and confidence.

The competition was expecting to tear us apart and steal most of our customers. They went to our customers and told them that we did not have materials, we did not have machines, we did not have experienced people to carry on, and we would not be able to provide an uninterrupted supply.

Dave realized that we had to keep our customers calm and confident that we would supply them and not let them down. Dave spent most of his time with the customers in these first few months. We kept the same prices, but we gave them better delivery dates.

For example, I received a call from Dave. "Eric, can we make this order in three days? Can you find material for it? Please check and call me back in ten minutes. I'm with the customer in Toronto, and he will give me the order if we promise the delivery in three days."

In ten minutes, I called him back.

"Dave, I'm putting a third shift on the CNC, which is our bottleneck. On Sunday we will do maintenance of the CNC so it won't break down. As for the material, I will use a new combination of thick and thin wooden parts in such a construction that the thickness will be the same and the number of glue and wood layers will be the same, so the strength will be the same. We have the material in stock. Our pressing capacity is okay. Yes, we can do it. Take the order."

Later the same day, Dave called me from his hotel room. "Eric, if we can do this, we can take many orders from our customers in Toronto. You see, they can take extra orders only if they can deliver on time in a week. That means we have to deliver in maximum three days." Dave was excited and happy.

We proved our competitors wrong. These were great times. We were like brothers. We worked practically fourteen or fifteen hours per day; we were going home just to sleep and recover our strength. In these first couple of years, 1994 and 1995, it was my wife who took care of the kids and me. She supported me with her courage, dedication, and love.

Renee started working at the company at the end of 1995 doing engineering work. She designed the molds and made drawings for the parts in AutoCAD. In the beginning, she was occupied with engineering and janitorial work at the office as well. She worked very hard and as in everything she has done, she was very efficient; she did not pick her head up for conversations or to have a break. She pushed me to give her new projects before she was done with what she was doing. Our lunches were short, only thirty minutes, and even then we were discussing the work. Renee started making 3D designs using AutoCAD and MasterCam, which was very advanced engineering at the time.

She was a very good, talented, and hardworking engineer, but Dave didn't see this; for almost a year, he kept her salary at the minimum level as the new workers in the factory were starting. I told him that she was doing things that very few engineers could do, but he did not believe me.

The main reason for that was that Renee, when she was working, was never sure she could do it. I understood her well. She would accept something as done only if it were perfect. She had always been a perfectionist in everything she was doing. In this new world of emigration, she was shy and not self-confident. This got worse when she was pressured to speak. She didn't speak well in French or English. She thought that every engineer in Canada and the United States could do what she was doing with ease—and maybe better than she.

This was driving me crazy, and I couldn't change the situation for a long time.

One day we were at the Atlanta International Woodworking Fair when we came across an AutoCAD booth specialized for furniture. I challenged Dave, saying that they would not know how to make 3D designs of irregular (not square) forms using the latest version of AutoCAD.

I had with me drawings of complicated furniture parts designed by Renee on AutoCAD.

When Dave spoke with them, they said it was impossible on AutoCAD. Dave was embarrassed.

The next day when we came back to Ottawa, he doubled Renee's salary. Still, that salary was lower than what a good engineer should be receiving, but at least she was recognized now as a capable engineer.

Dave did not want to repeat the same mistakes as his father by putting all his assets under one company. We saw the domino effect and how one bad department could easily bring down everything else if they were connected.

Dave's father, Avedis, lost everything at the end. His kids, Robert and Dave, were taking care of him and their mother, Armine.

Avedis was a proud man. Soon after that, he got sick; a few years later, he passed away.

We told ourselves to be careful and not to do too many different things at the same time, to concentrate on only one business—making wood components for office furniture.

We were very good in this business, and we proved it, soon becoming one of the best companies in this field in Canada and one of the preferred suppliers of wood components for office furniture in North America.

How easy it is to write this, but in reality, it was very difficult to get there and remain at the top for the next fifteen years.

I thank God that I had been given this chance, and I also thank God for the patience and courage and love of my family.

I also thank God that Dave was an honest man; he kept his word till the end of our business relationship. I'm proud we managed well till the end.

We continued being good partners, but I was always afraid to even wonder how I could one day leave the company. With every year, a good part of the profits were reinvested back in the company so the value grew, but I could get my real share value only if we sold the company together or I reached the age of sixty-five. However, Dave kept my salary the same as his till almost my last paycheck. I have to give him full credit for this.

As the years passed, the company grew. We couldn't keep everything in the same building, so we rented a separate one, where we stored the raw materials and prepared them for the orders.

In 1997, we opened a new factory, where I was the CEO of the company.

The company specialized strictly in producing exposed parts. Exposed parts are all those parts where the wood is visible. At Seda Inc., we produced the upholstered parts. This separation between exposed and upholstered products actually helped to improve the quality, implement new processes, and train workers and managers for these two different types of wood components. The downside was that the materials were coming to the two factories from a third place, so there was transportation cost and delays. Also, if everything were under one management in one bigger building, we could have some savings in the overhead and space costs.

After three or four years, the factory that made exposed parts grew faster; we could not continue to operate in the same building. Seda started having problems since a bigger part of my time was dedicated to the new factory. We had to move again. It was time to look around for a much bigger building, where we could put everything together.

In the beginning of 2001, we bought our industrial building.

At the end of the winter, we moved everything to one location; all this was done without any interruption in the production. Our clients did not feel anything.

Dave and I made a decision to keep Seda and the building as separate companies.

I invested all my family savings during the last six years' work at Seda in this building. This was a good investment and a good decision. The other option was to invest alone in a building with apartments. This for sure would have deteriorated my relationship with Dave.

Soon after that, we started a paint shop in the same building, but as a different company.

By 2001 ten years had passed since we came to Canada. I had worked very hard and was under constant stress.

I was getting tired. I needed help in my work.

My partner, Dave, was five years younger than I and considerably more ambitious.

It was not easy for him either. Dave was the president of Seda and the building, and he kept control of all the assets. He wanted to make Seda bigger, but at the same time, he was afraid to hire more people in the management and in the engineering.

"We cannot afford more people in the overhead. This will make our company not profitable," Dave argued.

"Dave, I'm getting tired, and I need people to help me. Either we have to keep the company the same size, or we need to hire new capable people so we can support the growing of Seda," I rebutted.

"You are the vice president of manufacturing and product development. You have to find solutions, but keeping the company the same size or making it smaller is out of the question," Dave said.

Four more years passed, and in 2005, I turned fifty years old.

It was a very difficult year for me.

We were working long hours, with few short breaks and with high intensity. Dave and I had a variety of responsibilities, and we overlapped each other when needed.

I was starting to get more and more tired and was thinking about retirement, while Dave wanted to start new companies, open new businesses, and grow the existing ones. It was getting increasingly obvious that we had different goals.

In 2004, we opened a new factory under Seda Inc. in the United States. Every week, we had to visit the plant in Chicago, Illinois.

We took turns going to our plant in Illinois. One week I went, and the next week it was Dave's turn. We had to make sure that both factories were running well. Every Monday or Tuesday, we took the first early flight in the morning at 6:00 a.m. from Ottawa to Chicago. We stayed usually for three days. On Wednesdays or Thursdays at 5:00 p.m., we took flights to Ottawa, with one stop in Detroit, Michigan, Cleveland or Cincinnati, Ohio, or sometimes Newark in New Jersey. We arrived home in Ottawa sometimes at eight o'clock, sometimes at midnight, and we had to be at work the next day at the factory at 8:00 a.m. On Saturdays, we had to go to work again so we could catch up with the work and prepare for the next week.

I was getting tired, and I told Dave that we needed to find a permanent manager or close our Seda Inc. factory in the United States.

I remember the summer of 2005, when Dave was in Las Vegas to visit a show. I was in our factory in Chicago. Dave bought me a ticket going to Ottawa, with a stop in Las Vegas for twelve hours.

Dave called me in my office in Chicago. "Eric, stay for a day with me, so you can have a quick look at Las Vegas. We will have a nice dinner in a good restaurant, and then you can take the red-eye flight at 10:30 p.m. from Las Vegas to Ottawa. You can be at Seda for work tomorrow morning at 8:00 a.m.," Dave said.

Although I had just turned fifty years old, I was feeling much older.

I arrived at the airport in Las Vegas at 9:30 a.m. I had a terrible headache, and I first went to the restroom to wash my face. When I looked in the mirror, I saw myself looking ten years older than I was. My eyes were red, and right below one of them, I saw a nickel-sized black spot. The capillary had burst and caused the black spot. At this moment, I realized that this could also happen in my brain. I was not scared, but just tired. I realized that I could not do that for too long, but I was not ready to stop working and Dave was not ready to replace me.

I had to talk to him and tell him that my plans were to retire in five years.

I met with Dave in the garden of the hotel. He was just finishing his breakfast.

I joined him for a coffee. The whole morning and after lunch till about five o'clock, we were visiting different hotels and enjoying the beauty of the architecture and design of the hotels in Las Vegas.

We walked around Las Vegas from one hotel to another. It was very hot outside, and fresh and cool inside the hotels. We stopped to rest at the bars and bistros, where we drank glasses of wine. I was tired, and the alcohol began making me dizzy.

Dave was trying to make me start talking about my plans for the future.

I was kind of afraid to start talking about it, knowing well that this might trigger a quick end of my work at Seda. I was not ready for this, but at the same time, I was tired and it was not right for Dave not to know.

At 6:30 p.m., we went to a nice restaurant for diner.

We started eating, but Dave did not wait to finish the supper and started talking.

"Eric, we need to have a brainstorm about the future of Seda." Dave became very serious.

"How do you see Seda in a few years? What direction do we need to take? What are your personal plans as well? I need to know so I can make the right decisions." Dave sat straight in his chair as he asked all these questions.

When I didn't say anything, he continued, "Sometimes it is very hard to get out of you what you think. We need to talk, and I really need your input."

The time had come for me to say what I was thinking directly and without any more delays. I looked at the table full of rich dishes and crystal glasses filled with red wine and carefully put down my silver fork and knife.

"Dave, what I feel is that the future of Seda will be shifting from 60 percent upholstery products and 40 percent exposed to 25 percent upholstery and 75 percent exposed. I'm talking for our plant in Ottawa. I think we need to move the manufacturing of the low-grade, inexpensive products overseas to Singapore. Our supplier in Singapore is proving to perform well, and the quality is good. They can concentrate on supplying us with the upholstery parts, and at the same time, we can concentrate on improving our exposed parts manufacturing at Seda.

"I also do not see the future of our plant in Illinois. It did play a very important role in 2004, when we did not have the Singaporean plant and the Canadian dollar became stronger than the US dollar. It was also very important for us to be close to Illinois, Indiana, and Michigan, where we had many potential customers. Now, after almost two years, we have dominated the market, and we can continue supplying them from Ottawa and Singapore."

I stopped for a moment to clear my voice. Dave was looking at me and waiting for me to continue.

"Also, I'm getting tired running between the two factories. We were supposed to find a manager, but somehow we are not able to keep one.

"As for my personal plans, I believe I would like to go to an early retirement in five years. This will give you time to restructure the companies."

Dave did not say anything for the rest of the supper.

I took the flight to Ottawa the same night and went to work the next morning.

As the weeks passed, I noticed that Dave started going more often to Chicago, and I was going less; Dave was going three times per month, and me only once. A few months later, he was the only one going to Illinois—twice a month—till one day about a year after our brainstorming, he told me that it was time to close the factory in the United States.

In the meantime, Garo, the general manager of Seda, left the company. This was a new, old problem. This position had been changed three times in the last twelve years. We put in his place a young industrial engineer who had been with us already for three years—Gabriel.

Gabriel was a good Canadian-born fellow. He had graduated in industrial engineering. He was appropriate for this position. Even more important, he was easy to work with. At the time, he was about twenty-eight or twenty-nine years old. He liked working with me.

I helped him as much as possible to learn about the processes and become a good production manager. I helped him with the schedules and with a proactive approach to avoid problems by sharing information and experience about the products that were scheduled for production.

Every day at 10: 30 a.m., we had a production meeting with the key leaders of the factory departments and the engineers. We went over all new entered orders, and at the end, the shipping schedule for the week. For the last part of the meeting, only the production leaders were involved, and the engineers were released to go back to their work. This time was used for the key people in the company to know what was going on and what was coming and to prepare for difficult items, as well as exchange information between the production and engineering departments.

Dave hoped that Gabriel would learn and start doing these meetings himself without my involvement—at least not every day.

Dave asked Gabriel to communicate with the customers. Customers were calling him all the time, and he had to take the calls. These conversations were taking more than half of his time. This responsibility, combined with his responsibility of general production manager, made him very busy.

Time passed quickly month after month and year after year. After three years had passed, Gabriel certainly had learned many things, but still he was not able to become a strong, independent production manager.

The formula Dave and I used worked well for many years; however, things were slowly changing to new unknown values and parameters, which Dave had to explore.

The balance was changing, and Dave was getting more and more inpatient to find a new way of balancing and managing the company without me.

He expected Gabriel to take more responsibility and be able to do much more.

I was still very busy, and this was driving Dave crazy.

One Saturday morning in the spring of 2010, about five years after our conversation in Las Vegas, Dave came to see me. I was alone in the office.

"Good morning! How are you, Eric?" Dave smiled and sat down in front of my desk.

"Good morning. I'm fine. How are you?" I smiled back.

"I need to talk about your plans. Are you going to stay, or are you going to leave? You understand that it is not easy to find somebody who will have your experience, knowledge, and willingness to work the same way as we both do. At the same time, if I bring somebody on, you have to practically show him everything you do, and it may take at least six months before he will be ready, if he ever becomes ready. But once he is ready, you understand I cannot have two vice presidents"

"Well, Dave, we both somehow avoid talking about this, but yes, I understand what you mean." I cleared my voice and continued.

"I might stay longer, or even stay till age sixty-five, if you hire, and more importantly keep, more people in new positions. I see recently you have started hiring more people in a few new positions, as I have been asking you for many years. You hired Vartan this year; his main goal is to learn everything I know about processes of manufacturing and be able to lead tests in the pressing department. You also hired a new person for the purchasing of materials and spare parts, and John for making the quotations and learning how to place orders to our overseas supplier for ready panels and cut-to-size parts. All this is finally something that is actually helping me. As you know, I was involved directly in all of it."

"Yes, but you are still busy," Dave said, looking down at his feet.

"I'm not pretending to be busy. There is still a lot of work to be done in the company, especially when you are growing the company. I'm still involved in production helping Gabriel; since he is too busy, I still help the new guys to learn and organize their jobs. I still have to take care of product development and maintenance of the machines, finding ways to cut costs or keep the costs down in manufacturing. I'm busy fixing quality problems and making sure the customers are comfortable with the ways we implement improvements. I convince them that mistakes will not happen again." I stopped for a moment, looking at Dave and giving him a chance to say something.

"Anyhow, I need you to give me a final answer by the end of your vacation. When you come back from Bulgaria, you have to tell me whether you are staying or leaving. If you decide to leave, then I will need you to stay for at most probably six to nine more months."

He slowly stood up, smiled in a friendly fashion, and left the office.

But at this moment, I felt that he did not want me in his company.

This was my company also, and any success and achievement was due to both of us. We did this together, and now I felt—just for a short time—that he was looking for ways to push me out.

But after all, didn't I tell him five years earlier that I wanted to retire? Yes, I did. The right question is why? I was getting overworked and tired, so this was for me the only way to tell him to hire more people or I would be forced to leave.

My wife had worked for fifteen years before stopping. She had no more energy to keep up with the speed of the new projects. The last year she had to do her engineering job and learn how to implement a new engineering product, Solid Work, at the same time. She had been under too much stress for a long period, and she became sick and depressed. I had to stop her working before she became too sick.

Dave had five years to make his choice about me, and now it looked like he had made it without saying it, as if it were going to be my choice.

He never said I had to leave. He was very good at making people work hard. I agreed with him that this was very important for the success of the company. I guess this is the standard in this world. I have accepted it.

If you can no longer work very hard and deliver what is expected from you, you lose your job.

Maybe you have to be like that to be successful in a business. Dave was a good businessman!

Once, at the end of a conversation about us, he told me, "We haven't changed, Eric. We are the same; just with age, now our priority is different."

I did not make any comments, and I still think about what he said.

But at the same time, he had done so many good things for me and my family since we started working together. Nobody else would have done as much as he did. We couldn't have achieved as much as we did if he were not next to us every day. He was always there for me and my family if we needed something. I learned my English talking with him and my colleagues at the company. I saw the new world in Canada and the

United States, and I understood it better through his eyes and his experience and knowledge. I learned how to manage a dynamic company and how to deal with the suppliers and the customers. Dave and my wife, Renee, have been the booster that brought the best out in me.

He remained one of my closest friends, even in the last year when things were not going well anymore. He helped my daughter Nevy when she was pregnant to start working temporarily at Seda Inc. in the office as an accountant assistant.

❧

"Are you sleeping?" Renee was shaking Eric's hand. "You are in the sun, and you are going to get burned."

Eric stood up. It was getting hot, and he felt the fresh breeze from the sea.

"I'm going to swim. Do you want to come with me?" Eric asked and took her hand, helping her up.

They swam in the refreshing waters of the sea. On their way out, he saw somebody paddling a sea canoe-kayak. He loved canoeing.

"Do you mind if I rent a canoe for an hour?" Eric asked.

"Okay, but do not get too far, like the last time in Dominican Republic."

"All right, I'll stay in view. I need to get some exercise." Eric kissed her and went down the beach to check where he could get one of those canoe-kayaks.

The sea was calm, and only small waves were reminding him that he was paddling in the Black Sea and not in a lake. He looked back at the beach and saw his wife waving at him. He smiled and waved to her. He decided to go about two hundred meters offshore and follow the coastline from there away from the swimmers. The sun was high, and he kept on his sunglasses, his golf hat, and an orange life jacket, which he hated but was obliged to wear.

Soon he forgot where he was; he was just paddling and did not notice that he had passed the two hundred meters a long time ago.

Their vacation in the beautiful resort at Sunny Beach was almost over, but he hadn't made up his mind.

Shall I stay, or shall I go? He was thinking and trying to come to a reasonable decision.

Last week they went to Sofia to see their relatives.

Eric had discussed his problems with his uncle Ed, Alexa, her husband Dinko, and their son, Boris, as well.

Uncle Ed had an active corporate experience. He used to be a vice president of a big corporation with twenty-seven factories all over Bulgaria before he retired in the 1990s.

Dinko was a smart businessman with international experience. He had been a representative of an American machinery company for Eastern Europe and Africa. He helped build new factories in Croatia, Bosnia, Bulgaria, Greece, Ukraine, Turkey, Azerbaijan, and South Africa.

Boris was part of the new generation of very successful and capable young businessmen in Bulgaria.

Boris had graduated from the American Business University in Bulgaria. After working for six months in London, he realized that he was wasting his time. The big company he worked for was not taking him seriously. He had good ideas and was full of energy.

Boris went back to Sofia with the idea to start his own business together with three of his friends, colleagues from the ABU. In 2002, they founded a software company.

In 2004, their company was chosen as the best employer in Bulgaria. The next year, the company was selected as the fastest-growing software company in Eastern Europe. They were chosen to be the preferred software supplier for Microsoft for Eastern Europe. When Eric was talking to Boris that night, the company already had about 250 specialists working at five offices in five different countries At the Bulgarian office in Sofia, which was the largest, employees were earning on average the top private salaries in Bulgaria. Most importantly, they all were treated with respect and felt they were part of the success of this international company.

Regardless of the success, Boris was a calm, modest young man, with a handsome smile. But do not get the wrong idea: these young men were sharp, and they had surrounded themselves with very good specialists and lawyers in Bulgaria and internationally.

Eric realized that his relatives had been listening to him, understood his problems, and supported him with words, advice, and ideas.

They made him feel much better and confident that he could find a solution.

"I need to talk now with my wife and make a final decision," Eric said loudly while still paddling.

Cold water from a big wave splashed on his body.

Eric looked around, and the first thing he saw was that the sea was getting rougher. Then he looked for the beach, but he could see only the tall hotels on the coast.

"That is not possible. When did I come here?"

He looked at his watch. Only forty-five minutes had passed since he started paddling. He tried to calm down and evaluate the situation. He was probably about two to three kilometers into the sea. The problem was that there was a current sucking him in. Otherwise he couldn't get so far just with paddling. He had to first fight the panic.

"Calm down! *Calm down!*" He stopped paddling and watched for the sea current and the wind. His instincts and energy came back in full force.

"Yes, the current is taking me to the east, so if I try to fight it, I will soon get tired and might not be able to make it out. There should be another way."

He looked at the big bay of Sunny Beach. It was in the shape of a horseshoe. To the north about four to five kilometers was the nose Eminee, where the mountain dove into the Black Sea. The wind was coming from there, from the north. To the south about five kilometers away was the peninsula of the old city of Nessebar.

"That is my goal," Eric said, confident of his decision. "I will be with the wind and paddling on a forty-five-degree angle with the current. I should be there in less than an hour.

He started paddling, but this time he kept his concentration and put himself in a steady rhythm. The waves were bigger, but manageable. He was sure they would get smaller as he got closer to Nessebar.

He loved it. He felt he was again in charge. There was a beauty in the forces of nature.

"We have to learn how to respect nature, understand it well to be able to use it and not fight it. Then we will be stronger because we are part of this nature. Mother Nature will take care of us if we are with her!" Eric smiled and kept paddling.

He suddenly remembered when he and Dave went to New Brunswick on a three-day fishing trip. It was a year after they started their company. They were invited by their wood supplier. They wanted to visit the factory and then spend two days over the weekend fly-fishing salmon on the Miramichi River. Eric didn't have proper clothes and shoes. Dave took him to Walmart and bought the proper equipment for them.

It was still cold after the long Canadian winter, but it was so beautiful on the river. The owner of the wood factory organized a one-day trip down the Miramichi River with canoes. They were eight people in four canoes. Dave and Eric were put together in a canoe, and the local guys took the other three canoes. They explained how to paddle, how to avoid shallow waters where the stream is fast, and to look ahead for more calm waters. A guy was waiting for them fifteen miles down the river, with two cars parked at a log house.

When they were alone in the canoe, Dave asked Eric, "Have you done this before?"

"No. I have paddled with a canoe on Lake Esterel up northeast of Ottawa and once on Lake Memphremagog in the Estrie region of southern Quebec. I love nature, and I understand her language," Eric said, smiling.

Dave looked at him, not understanding a word, but trusting him.

"So, what do I do?" he asked.

"Just trust the river, and do not be afraid. Follow the river; do not fight him. Look far ahead for big obstacles. If we miss our goal, do not fight it, but go with the river. The water will push us back from the big stones. Most importantly, stay low in the canoe so the center of gravity will be low. You are heavier than me, remember. If we get caught in shallow rapid waters, you have to lie down on the bottom of the boat to spread your weight evenly, and I will keep the canoe within the stream— nothing more, nothing less."

"Are you sure this is your first time?" Dave asked him.

"I'm not sure how, but I know what I have to do. Just trust me."

Later in the log house, Dave and Eric were the only ones whose canoe did not turn over. The local guys were wet and shaken from the icy waters of the river, where they fell and struggled to get back in the canoes.

They all laughed and drank whisky to get warm and kept their backs against the fireplace in the log house. None of them believed that this was Dave and Eric's first time on a river.

On this trip, Dave and Eric learned how to trust each other's abilities. They also learned one more, very important lesson: do not fight the river. Use it!

❧

Eric looked at his watch. He was right. It took him forty minutes to get close to the coast of Nessebar. Here he turned the canoe and started following the coastline back inside the bay, heading to the center of the horseshoe arc, where Renee was waiting for him. He was worried for her. God knows what she was thinking happened to him.

The sun was going down in the west and it was about four thirty when he finally arrived.

Renee was there waiting for him. She was upset and relieved at the same time. "What happened?" she cried out.

"Is that how you stay in view? Where have you been? I was so worried for you." She hugged him.

"I'm sorry. I didn't realize how fast the time had passed, and by the way, I stayed in view all the time. I was able to see the top of the hotels all the time." Eric was smiling at her.

He continued, "Hey, I'm hungry as a wolf. Let's go home to change, and then let's go to a restaurant. I'm all yours for the rest of the day and the night. I'm ready to discuss with you what our decision will be." He kissed her, and then he went to return the canoe-kayak. This was something he knew was not going to be very pleasant. They had given him instructions to come back in an hour and not to go too far in the sea.

June 2011

One more year passed, and many things happened.

Most importantly, Eric and Renee became grandparents. Their daughter Nevena had a son, Krassi, in February 2011. It was something wonderful and brought happiness to all of them. The whole family gathered together. Maya came from Victoria to meet with her nephew, Krassimir. The old grandparents Nikola and Nina were the happiest. Their dream came through to see a great-grandson. Nikola was sick with cancer, but he was feeling good and now he was smiling—something the family hadn't seen for a long time.

In February, Eric told Dave that he would contact his lawyer to discuss details about the dissolution of their partnership.

In June, Eric and Dave signed all the necessary documents in front of the two lawyers without going to court. As Emma, Dave's wife, said, "This is an uneventful and boring separation." For Eric and Dave, this actually meant a lot. They both made great efforts and compromises, and they both hoped to remain good cousins and friends.

At the end of June, their daughter Maya came again from Victoria to see her grandparents and her sister, Nevena, her husband, Antony, and their son, Krassi, before Eric and Renee went on vacation in Bulgaria.

It was a beautiful summer morning in Ottawa. Maya was making tea when Eric went to the kitchen.

"Good morning, Maya. Did you have a good sleep? Are you hungry?"

"No, I'm not hungry, at least not when I have just awakened."

"Well, it is already ten o'clock," he said.

"No, for me it is just seven o'clock," Maya answered.

"Why do you not change your clock? Now you are in Ottawa."

"Because I need to work with my customers in Victoria, and so I keep it on my time." She was getting a bit inpatient with her father, something new Eric and Renee noticed.

Maya had changed since she moved to Victoria. She started thinking that she knew more than her parents, and she had very little patience with her parents asking questions or trying to give her advice.

Eric felt he needed to change the subject.

"Maya, today I had something happen to me that I will not forget for a long time."

She looked up with curiosity. "What was it, Dad?"

"I went to the office as usual on Saturday to check on my e-mails and feed my fish, and I saw on the side of the building the parked car of one of the employees. This was the car of our mechanic, Sevak.

"Do you want me to continue?" Eric asked his daughter, noticing that she had turned her back to him as she checking her messages.

"Yes, yes, I'm listening," Maya said, putting away her Blackberry and picking up the mug with tea instead.

"Okay," Eric said and went on. "After a while I decided to go in the back of the factory and say hello to Sevak, as I did every Saturday. He was behind the machines, working and singing an Armenian song. When he saw me, he came out, greeted me, and asked, 'Do you want a cup of coffee? I prepared a pot in the cafeteria.'

"'Yes, I do,' I said, and we went to the cafeteria in the office.

"'Eric, I want to ask you something,' Sevak said in Armenian since he didn't speak English or French very well.

"My Armenian is good in understanding, but weak in speaking. So I always replied in single words or simple sentences.

"'Yes, with pleasure.'

"'Eric, I understand that you are retiring, and you will not be coming in anymore. Is that true? Why are you leaving?'

"I did not know how to find words in Armenian to explain it. He waited for a minute and then continued talking, but this time in perfect Russian. All Armenian immigrants from Yerevan speak very good or perfect Russian.

"'You know I will miss you a lot. You are a good person.' His eyes turned red. He took a deep breath and continued again quickly, as if somebody were going to stop him. 'There are very few really good people I know in this world, and you are one of them. I have known you since I came to work at Seda, and you were always there for me and everybody else who needed something. You came every morning to shake my hand and ask me how I am. Your smile boosted my morale, and I looked forward to it every day: Parev, *inch pesses?* Good morning. How are you?'

"Sevak continued, 'When I was telling you my problems, you always listened to me, and most of the time, you did something for me to help me. You did the same for everybody in the company.

"'Slowly the years passed by, and now I have worked for you more than twelve years, and I have only good memories about you. I do not have enough words to express my sadness. I wish God to give you and your family a lot of health and happiness.'

"By now my eyes were turning red, and my throat was dry. I coughed, cleared my voice, and started speaking slowly in Russian, carefully choosing my words. 'You don't have to say anything more, Sevak. Thank you! I know what you mean.'

"'How is your wife doing? Is she working?' I asked, trying to change the subject.

"'She is okay. Yes, she is working in a sewing company on the east side of Ottawa, but she is not receiving a paycheck. She is being paid cash, and very little. I tried to stop her, but she insists on doing what she can for the family.'

"'I know, Sevak. This is the life of emigrants. Most of us do not know how to speak proper French or English, so we have to accept any work and be grateful for it. We do not have any choice but to accept our destiny so our kids can be more successful. I'm sure your son can speak in both French and English. He will be luckier than you both. Now your grandchildren, they are the real Canadians. They will speak perfect English, French, and Armenian. They will have their full education in Canada and full opportunities to achieve much more than we did.'

"'Are you coming to work next week?' he asked me.

"'Yes, I will be here on Monday morning,' I said, without knowing for sure if Dave was going to ask me to stay longer.

"'I'll see you then—and I thank you for the coffee,' I added.

"'*Anush alla!* [Let it be sweet!]'

"'Sevak, I'm happy to be able to see the beauty of the simple things around us. Not everybody has eyes to see them and the heart to feel them. It makes me happy that I did not lose this ability. Thank you again for your friendship.'

"Sevak was truly moved, and he just stood up, turned his head, and went back to work.

"I did the same, but this time I came home followed by my thoughts and emotions."

Maya pulled Eric out from his memories. "Dad, you will miss the work and the people you worked with, but you need to take a long vacation," she said. "I know how difficult it's been for you, especially the last six months since you told Dave you want to retire."

July 2011

Eric and Renee arrived in Bulgaria late on the night of July 4, 2011.

The first day they spent together with Lisa and Arak. It was Lisa's birthday.

They went to a restaurant in Central Park in Plovdiv. It was fun, and they had a very good time. Afterward, they bought ice creams and walked the main street up to the old city of Plovdiv.

It was mindboggling to imagine that people lived here thousands of years ago.

They went on top of the hill and listened to the wind blowing through the old marble ruins of this ancient Roman theater, lighted by the same stars as a few thousand years ago.

This was one of the oldest places in the world where people lived. Some of their children decided to stay and continue the legacy of this gorgeous city.

They were born here and grew up here. Eric and Renee moved to Canada searching for a better life, but every year they returned to this place in the old city, as if to attend a religious ceremony—or as if this were part of their life, and maybe it was.

They had never broken the string keeping them attached to this land, these people, their history and culture. And why should they?

༃

It was time to see Aunt Vera.

Eric called her, and the next morning, he walked the streets of Plovdiv to her house.

He looked around at the old houses and trees. He looked at the people passing by. He looked at Bunargika Hill, where the statue of Aleusha was still standing. This was a monument built during the communist time. It symbolized the unknown Russian soldier.

Eric had a strange feeling that he actually never left Plovdiv. He felt the same warm and strong feeling for the city as if he had never left for Canada.

He passed a new big modern building with glass walls next to the old hotel Leipzig, where the hill Marcovo Tepe had been. This was a new mall, named after the hill. It was supposed to be a very modern and beautiful mall; Eric had read about it in the newspapers. There were underground garages, many famous stores, and even a cinema center and food court. Western culture was gaining a place in the country.

At the corner there was a small fruit store; Eric remembered it. He stopped and bought 2 kg of peaches for his aunt. These Bulgarian peaches were so juicy and so sweet. He missed them so much in Ottawa.

Finally he was in front of his aunt's house. The front door was open. She was waiting for him.

Aunt Vera was happy to see her nephew, but she was at the same time sad and alone. Magdalena and Victoria, her two daughters, had left Bulgaria to follow their destiny and look for their happiness in different faraway places.

Victoria was married to Lucco in Switzerland, and Magdalena was in Cyprus with her boyfriend.

Victoria's children, Tony and Vera, were married and living in Plovdiv. They had their own kids. However, Aunt Vera was feeling alone. Everybody had their own responsibilities, and they were busy with their own lives.

Tony, her grandson, was working as a supervisor at a German company, manufacturing refrigerators. Aunt Vera said that he was very capable in everything he was doing and his boss was happy with him.

Little Vera, Tony's sister, turned into a beautiful woman. Vera looked like her mother Victoria, but her eyes were surprisingly green. She had two twin charming boys. She took very good care of them without complaining or asking for help.

Times were difficult in the world. It was difficult to find a job in every part of the world. It was the same in Bulgaria, but there it was even more difficult. Many young people left the country looking for jobs in other parts of Europe, even in faraway countries like Canada and the United States. Almost a million Bulgarians had left to pursue their luck in foreign places. It was not easy for them nor was it easy for those who stayed, but it was very difficult for the old parents and grandparents, who had to survive on very small pensions in Bulgaria.

My aunt Vera lived alone, but she was not completely alone. Her daughters and grandchildren did not forget her and helped her regularly with some money. Most generous was her brother Edwin.

"How are you doing, Aunt Vera?" Eric asked after kissing her on the cheeks. "One more year passed by, and we again came to Bulgaria for our vacation."

She was smiling. She was happy to see him.

"Come in, Eric. Come, have a seat." She closed the door after him and slowly started walking inside the house. Eric was waiting for her, standing next to the chair.

"I feel tired, my back is hurting me a lot, and I have a hard time walking around."

"You have to walk, Aunty. That will keep you in better shape. Do you go out for walks?"

Aunty went straight to the kitchen. She did not hear him. She was preparing a coffee for him in the kitchen, so he went to join her. She was bent over a small table placed next to the sink and was filling two cups with thick, good-smelling coffee. Next to her, he saw two plates with cakes and burrecks. She knew he loved them, and she had prepared them for him.

"Oh, Aunty Vera, you prepared so many good things for me. Thank you; I really appreciate it."

"It's my pleasure, Eric. You know how much I love you."

He took the two coffees to the living-room coffee table, then came back to the kitchen and helped her with the plates as well. She came to sit next to the coffee table in the living room.

"I feel so lonely, Eric. I miss my daughters, especially now Magdalena."

"I see. She was coming to see you every day ..."

"No, she was not coming every day, but she was calling me every day, and I knew she was here and if I needed her, she would come right away."

"I know what you mean, but you have Tony and Vera and the little ones ..."

"Yes, and I love them, but it is difficult for me to go see them and they are busy," his aunt said, biting her lips.

"I got word Vera started working. Bravo! Good for her; she was able to find a job."

"Well, her job is to clean and cook at a rich family's house. I'm not very happy about this," she said with pain, again biting her lips.

She continued, "I did this when I retired and we did not have enough money. Remember, I went to the

States—New Jersey—for a year to help in the house of a rich Armenian family. They were very nice to me, but I know how it feels …"

"What are you talking about, Aunty? This is a job like any other job. It is better than staying home, or going out for a coffee with friends and complaining how difficult it is to find a job, but not doing anything about it."

"Nobody in my family wanted to study," his aunt said sadly. "Not Victoria, not Magdalena, not their children either. No matter how many times I asked them, they did not want to continue their education at the university."

She stopped for a moment and then continued.

"I wanted to go to the university so much, but at that time when I was young, only your father, Santo, was working and supporting our parents and your uncle Ed, who was at the university. There was no more money left for my education, even though I was so good in school. Then I got married to your uncle Manuk, and we had to work and take care of our family. Manuk was not a big fan of schooling either, so he did not support my desire to go to the university—and then the children came."

She stopped for a moment and passed both her hands through her white, thin hair.

Eric was listening to her and understood her feelings and worries.

Changing the subject, Vera asked, "Tell me about you. How are Nevena and the baby? Where are they now?"

"Oh, they are also here in Plovdiv. First, they went to Barcelona, where they stayed about a week with a cousin of Antony's father." He stopped for a moment and then continued, "Nevena and the baby, Krassi, are staying with Antony's parents, Rumina and Krassi."

Vera smiled and said, "I can imagine how happy they are now with Nevena, Antony, and little Krassi with them."

"Yes, they are! We are also very happy!" Eric said. "I told you that I knew Antony's mother, Rumina, since we were kids. We were friends when we were young. She was my neighbor in Plovdiv, and my family knew hers. Antony comes from a good family on both sides, and it looks like they love Nevena," he added.

"Yes, I know them also. It's a very good family," Vera agreed.

"How long do mothers take maternity leave from work in Canada?" Vera surprised him, changing the conversation so suddenly.

"I do not know exactly—maybe nine months, or maybe twelve. I will ask Renee; she knows better. Why?"

"I'm just curious. How is Maya doing? She couldn't come?"

"No, she couldn't, but she took a few vacation trips during the last year. Once to Hawaii and once to Mexico, so that was enough for her this year.

"Maya has been in Victoria for two years now. Things are not going well with her boyfriend, Marc, and we do not know how long she will stay there. He is a good man. Very professional in his work as a financial advisor, but he is too busy at his work and his hockey games. I guess it's a difference in culture. She is taking it very hard." Eric slowed down as he talked, as if he were picturing her difficulties.

"Anyhow, we will be happy if Maya comes back to Ottawa. We miss her. She is doing well with her business, but she is not happy without friends and family there."

"Yes," Vera agreed. "It is better if she is close to you in Ottawa. Now she has a nephew, one more member of the family. I hope she will meet somebody from the same culture—Bulgarian, Armenian, or Greek. It will be easier for her, and you as well."

"I know, but it is not easy for young women and men to get married. There are more things to do now than when we were young. And also, now they want to continue having fun for as long as they can without having responsibilities. Marriage is a big responsibility. I hope for her to meet the right person and them both to love each other. Marriage is happiness as well."

Eric stopped talking for a moment, finishing the cookies and sipping from the coffee.

"Aunty Vera, I wanted to tell you that I'm trying to write a book about our family and our emigrant life in Canada. It will include stories about our grandparents and their emigration as well from Turkey to Bulgaria," Eric said and stopped to see his aunt's reaction.

71

"This is good. I also wanted to preserve the stories of my mother and father," she said while looking in front of her at something only she was seeing.

"I wanted to preserve all these sad stories about leaving their homes and country during the First World War and the Armenian genocide. They were lucky to survive," his aunt said, and then she looked up in his eyes.

"How do you plan to write this book?" Vera asked.

"Well, I started it two years ago when I came back from our vacation in Bulgaria. At least I started putting down some thoughts. However, I did not write much. I was so busy with my work, and it took all my energy and concentration. But now that I'm no longer a partner with Dave and I'm not actively working, I can spend more time with the book," Eric explained.

Vera was listening to Eric with interest. She was smiling while waiting for him to continue.

"I had this idea for a long time to write a book that would mix our lives with stories of our grandparents, parents, and us. This is a book for all of us—old and new emigrants and their children—who faced problems and difficulties." Eric took a deep breath and continued.

"We had it all: love, sadness and happiness, despair and hope during two immigrations and between them. I want somehow to explain the difficulties our parents and relatives in Bulgaria had. At the same time, I want to write about the difficulties of our lives in a new country—Canada." Eric looked at his aunt to see if she was listening.

"In Canada, we had to start many things from scratch. We had to learn how to speak, how to write, how to drive, how to work in a foreign country," he said emotionally.

"I want to show how difficult and sometimes embarrassing it was learning to do simple things again, like a newborn. We had to learn how to take care of our kids, growing up now in a foreign country and culture ... It was like starting a new life. We now had chances to avoid old mistakes, but who could advise us not to make new ones? We were almost alone ..."

Eric looked in front of him, not really seeing the objects, but imagining others that were not entirely visible yet.

"Aunty Vera, I wanted to ask you about your aunt Nicole, my grandfather's sister. Dave told me that she was not a very good woman. This is bothering me, and I wanted to know if that was true." He stopped to give enough time to his aunt to remember her aunt Nicole.

"No, Nicole was not a bad woman. She was well-educated, a beautiful woman. She was a complicated and ambitious person, and she liked to live in high society. She certainly demanded a lot of attention from her relatives. She had very high expectations for her children and thought this was the way to make them ambitious achievers in life," Vera said. She paused to remember more.

"Your grandfather's brother Harry helped them in the beginning when they had difficulties. Harry was often helping his sister Nicole and her husband when they had financial difficulties. In this period of their lives, they had many difficulties. Harry was a rich man, and often my father blamed him for not helping him financially." Vera was now remembering more details she had heard.

"Harry had bribed the right people in Istanbul, and he arranged for his family to leave Turkey." Vera was slowly remembering the stories of her family.

"At the same time, your grandfather, my father Agop, was mobilized in the Turkish Army at a time when the Turks were killing or deporting the Armenians and blaming it all on the war.

"He barely lived by deserting the army and running to Istanbul and then to Bulgaria. He had nothing with him and was sick with spot typhus. Hundreds of people were dying every day from the high fever caused by this disease." She spoke slowly, getting more emotional.

"Yes, I know the story. My grandfather told me the story many times, and I will write about it in the book," Eric said.

"Harry loved his sister Nicole, and often he helped her and her husband with money when they needed it," his aunt repeated. "However, he did not treat my father the same way," Vera added.

"What do you mean? Did he blame his brother for not giving him part of the family money?" Eric asked.

"I do not know. I'm just repeating what my father said every time he got his nervous attacks and felt sick."

"What was he sick from?" Eric asked.

"It is hard to explain, but what the doctors were saying was that he went through a lot of stress during the war, and also surviving typhus and the high fevers contributed to his condition."

His aunt stopped for a while, as if she was trying to remember something, and then she continued, "My mother told me once that his condition became worse when one day there was a fire in his shop.

"His helper was smoking, and somehow the pot with the glue got on fire. Agop jumped up from his place and threw the pot out the door, but at the same time, a woman was passing by, and the glue and the fire got on her. Thank God it was winter and she was wearing a coat, so only the coat was on fire. My father quickly took a blanket from his shop and threw it over the woman. He saved her, but after that for many nights he couldn't sleep and for many days couldn't work, shaking into awful nervous breakdowns.

"During these terrible days and weeks, my mom, Arakssi, and grandmother, Ovsana, sold everything valuable they had at home. Also, his brother Harry

75

came a few times and helped them with food and some money."

"Were you alive at this time?" Eric asked.

"No, it was your father, Santo, who was born in 1924. My brother Edwin was born in 1930, and I was born in 1934.

"The years passed by, and sometimes my father was better and sometimes not. When your father became fourteen years old, he started helping his father after school. Edwin was eight years old, and I was four years old. Your father learned everything about how to make shoes and how to buy materials and how to sell the shoes. He had no choice but to learn quickly because it was difficult to predict when my father was going to be sick again.

"My brother Santo became the man of the house when he was twenty years old and had come back from his military service. He lost his carefree manner and became very serious. It was difficult for him. When his father got his nervous attacks, he would shout at Santo and even ask him to leave the house and never come back.

"Santo was always calm and strong and stood there for all of us. He did not allow my father to raise a hand or voice to me or Edwin or my mom."

Eric lifted his hand to stop her.

"I'm sorry to interrupt you, but what did Santo say about his uncle not helping his father enough financially?" Eric returned to the topic from which his aunt was running away.

"Well, it was obvious that Harry, my uncle, came home with money from Turkey. He bought a house and a nice store on the main street of Plovdiv.

"It was a bit later when Agop came and joined them in the house. He stayed with them for a year or so, and then he rented a small shop where he made shoes. He left the house and rented the room on the second floor right above his shop.

"Soon after that, he got married to my mom, Arakssi, and the next year, 1924, Santo was born."

"How did he meet Mezmama [Grandmother] Arakssi?" Eric asked.

"One day she came to the shop door and called Agop.

"*Agop, egur hos hima!*'—'Agop, come here now!'

"Both my father and his helper came out since both had the same name. My mom was looking for the younger Agop. She was bringing him a message from his mother, who lived next door to her. My father was a handsome man, and at the time, he had the reputation as one of the best shoemakers in town. They fell in love, and soon after that, my father asked her hand from Grandma Ovsana. They had a small ceremony in the Armenian church, and then Mom moved in with my father."

Eric raised a hand again to bring her back to his original question.

"You did not answer me what my father did when Mezhairig Agop was saying that the family money stayed with his older brother."

"When your father was twenty years old, one day Harry came to see his brother Agop, who was again sick. On the way out when they were alone, Santo asked his uncle:

"'Uncle Harry, I would like to ask you one question if you don't mind. I've been holding it back, hesitating to ask or not, but now I can't keep it to myself. At least I want to hear what your answer will be.'

"Harry looked at the young Santo under his big hairy eyebrows and said nothing.

"After waiting awhile, Santo continued.

"'For years my father has repeated over and over when he was sick that he has not received his part from the family money. You helped your sister, but not your brother. What do you have to say about this?'

"'Your father is a crazy man. Do not listen to him!' Harry said angrily.

"He did not say anything else, and he walked away, not giving any chance for Santo to react to his words," Vera said.

"Santo never asked his uncle the same question again, and that story was put behind him," his aunt finished.

"Aunt Vera," Eric asked, "was my grandfather crazy?"

"No, he was not crazy! You know, sometimes between family members when we get very upset, we might say bad things as an expression of our frustration, but then we feel very bad about it," Vera said.

And then, as if she were feeling guilty to blame her uncle without giving him a chance to defend himself, she added, "Uncle Harry was not a bad man. During these times in Turkey and also for Armenian families coming from Turkey, the tradition was like that. The big brother took responsibility when the father died. He had to make sure they could survive and get out of Turkey. This cost almost all the money the family had. He had to take care of their mother and marry off his younger sister, Nicole; as for Agop, he was a man, and a man was supposed to take care of himself."

Vera stopped for a while, but then she felt she needed to defend her father as well, and she continued, "Our father, Agop, was not a crazy man ...! When he was sick, he behaved very unusually. He screamed that he was dying, and he asked for a doctor. When we did not call for a doctor, he cursed us, mostly your father. He called him bad names. He was crying and begging for help. He threatened us, and then he again begged for a doctor.

"When we called a doctor, the doctor said that he was okay; he just needed to calm down and get over this nervous attack.

"The sickness turned him to a weak man, who was afraid of many things. But was he really a weak man?" Vera asked a rhetorical question, trying to remember different stories.

"My mother told me that in 1928, when your father was four years old, there was a big earthquake, with the epicenter in Chirpan. Chirpan is about fifty kilometers east of Plovdiv. During this quake, many houses were destroyed, and there were many dead and wounded people.

"My mom told me that it was just about time to go to bed and they had put on their pajamas. Arakssi went to turn off the light, and she heard deep, strong noises coming from behind the door. She got scared and ran to close the door, but the door didn't fit the frame—and then she felt it. Strong waves of the quake shook the house.

"Before she turned to grab Santo, Agop ran by them on his way out, leaving her inside. Arakssi took Santo in her arms and ran after him out in the backyard. There, over a narrow corridor, was a big stone plate. The exit of the yard passed under this plate, so they had to run under it to go to the street. The plate was shaking and jumping up and down and was going to fall at any moment, but maybe the house was going to fall first and they were very close to it. They had to go out. Agop grabbed them both and forced them under the plate and out to the street. There, on the street, was a woman crying loudly that she had forgotten her small baby inside the house. She was asking her husband to go in after the baby, but he was paralyzed from the fear of the quake and not moving, holding in his hands two more children.

"Suddenly Agop, not saying a word, ran back under the jumping stone plate, into the backyard, and back into the house. There on the second floor was their neighbor's apartment. A few minutes later, he came out, holding in his hands a crying baby. He had barely passed under the plate when it jumped one last time and came crashing onto the ground. He gave the baby back to the woman, and then turned back to Arakssi, shaking himself again in his nervous attack."

Vera stopped for a moment. She was obviously remembering more events, and now she was smiling. Eric waited for her to continue, but she said something else. He let her just speak as her memories were coming and jumping from one thing to another. He was afraid to stop her.

"My mom, Arakssi, was able to write and read and speak fluently in Armenian, Turkish, and Bulgarian. She was a self-educated, intelligent woman. She loved reading books, and she loved telling us children stories. She believed in God. In her stories, the good always won over the bad. She was a good woman, filled with love for her family.

"Hardworking at home, she also helped Agop and Santo in their work making shoes.

"She always made time for us to sing her sad Armenian songs, and then she would play with us and make us laugh and play games. She told us how important it is to be a good person, to be honest and to help others when they need help.

"She told us to learn about the world and keep on studying, even if we did not go to school.

"She taught her husband, Agop, how to read and write in Bulgarian without his going to school there. Agop knew how to write and read in Turkish, Armenian, and even some Arabic. This knowledge saved his life in the army."

Eric was surprised and wanted to hear more about what had saved the life of his grandfather. "How come? I don't know this story. Can you tell me about it, please?"

Vera smiled. "I'm not sure if I know the whole story." She stopped for a while and then continued:

"This happened during the Greek-Turkish War in 1921, when Agop was taken into the army.

"One day his Turkish officer asked him if he knew Arabic. He said no. Then the officer smiled and said, 'I'm going to give you a recommendation to my colleague. He is an Arab, but a very good officer in our army. You will serve under his command on the front line against the Greeks in West Anatolia. He will take good care of you.'

"Later, as the train headed to the Greek front loaded with many other Turkish soldiers, Agop kept his right hand on his pocket over his heart, where he had put the closed letter. He was silently praying for the health of this good officer, who was so kind as to give him a recommendation letter. But at the same time, he had misgivings. He was hoping that his Turkish friend from the army camp was wrong. According to his friend, there was a plan against the Armenian solders to be sent to the most difficult places on the front line and killed there. His friend told him that the night before they were going to be sent by train to the front.

"'Nothing bad will happen to me,' Agop kept repeating to himself. Now he had this letter, and his officer was going to save his life. A few hours later, when the train was about 100 to 120 kilometers away from Istanbul, Agop asked for permission to go to the toilette. A sergeant escorted him to the door and said, 'Make it fast.'

"In the small room, he opened the letter and was shocked when he read the recommendation:

"'This Armenian *gjaur* [infidel] must be killed as soon as he gets to the front line.'

"My father had no choice. He opened the window and jumped out," Aunt Vera said.

"Yes, I know about that part of the story," Eric said, surprised about the letter and the cruelty and arrogance of this Turkish officer.

"Please continue. Maybe you know something else that I don't," Eric asked impatiently.

Vera narrated the story as her mind returned to her memories.

The train passed through a city not far from Adapazar—about 130 kilometers away from Istanbul—where Agop jumped off. He was lucky because he was born in this city and he grew up playing on the hills surrounding the city. He knew the forest and the paths running to the river. He knew the green fields, where for the first time he had kissed a girl, and the streets, where he played balls with the other boys. He remembered the Armenian school he had finished as a boy and the Turkish school where he studied as a teenager. He knew all the boys on his street, where his house was one of the best; he was proud of his father, mother, brother, and sister.

For the first time since being taken into the army, he felt safe and confident that he would run away. This was his place, where he felt protected. He was sure everybody would help him.

He ran for about an hour in the direction of Adapazar. When he was almost out of the forest, he decided to wait till the sun went down and then he would go into the city. He would ask one of his Turkish friends to help him with money and clothes so he could go to Istanbul and hide in the big capital. There nobody could find him, and then he would figure out what to do.

Why in the world did this bad officer want to kill him? He had not done anything bad to anybody. He considered himself as much Armenian as Turkish, and he was going to protect his country against foreigners. He was ready to fight for Turkey. He remembered all his Turkish friends at the school. For them, he even took the classes of the funny Arab teacher who was showing them the words from the Koran even though he was Christian. It did not bother him to learn from the Koran as well. The teacher loved him, and he learned some basic words in Arabic. He learned how to read and write words from the Koran. And now this knowledge had saved his life.

He was sure there was a terrible mistake, but he had to go to the big city and find a way to protect himself in court if necessary. The letter was in his pocket. He was not running away—he was not a deserter! He was just going to save his life from this crazy officer, and then he was ready to go back to the army if necessary.

The sun was going down, and soon he would take this path to the river and then turn on the big road going into the city. Suddenly he heard voices and then screams. In the beginning, he was not sure what it was. Soon he recognized some angry words in Turkish and some in Armenian.

Something was not right, and it sounded very threatening. He came to the edge of the forest, and from there he saw and heard something that made him feel sick. He saw—and even recognized—some men, whose hands were wired tightly together in a line. On both sides, he saw Turkish soldiers in dark olive uniforms holding rifles with bayonets. Then he saw in the far distance, where the city was, some running lights on the darkening sky, as if somebody had started big fires at the same time in many places.

Something was going really wrong, and he opened his eyes wider and looked back to the human shadows, not seeing very well now since the sun had just gone down in the forest. Now the voices and screaming were terrible. He couldn't take it anymore and ran back in the forest, far away from this nightmare.

He ran till he kicked a root of a tree and fell down. He stayed there, shaking from something he couldn't explain exactly. A long time after all the voices were gone, he decided to go back and check if he was not just dreaming. Was all of that really happening?

He remembered stories from his father and mother that when they were young, one day in 1890, something happened to their good Turkish neighbors. The neighbors turned on them, destroying their houses and killing people just because they were Armenians and Christians. Tens of thousands of Armenians were killed.

The Turkish Sultan Hamid stopped the violence and said that it was a mistake of some crazy people, fanatics. Turkish authorities promised all Armenians: "From now on, this will never happen again!"

Then he remembered 1915, when he was seventeen years old. His brother Harry was the man of the house after his father passed away.

One day the Turkish Army came and evacuated all the Armenians out of the city. They said this was for their own good—to be protected from the war and fanatic Muslims who might turn against the Christians.

There were about twenty thousand Armenians, according to his Armenian teacher, when they left the city; only four thousand came back three or four years later.

Thanks to his brother Harry, their family came back. They were nine people in the family when they left Adapazar, and they all came back. Harry was a very serious and smart man, and he found a way to protect his family. Harry negotiated with an officer to take them to an isolated Turkish village and help them settle there as a Turkish family. They stayed there till the end of the war, when it was safe to go back home.

When they came back to Adapazar, most of the Armenian houses were destroyed or already taken by Turkish emigrants from Greek and Bulgarian territories. Everybody was scared, and everybody had lost relatives. The stories were terrible.

Thousands of people from the Adapazar area died during this evacuation. There was no future for their family in Adapazar, so soon after that, they moved to Istanbul.

In Istanbul, it was not easy to survive either. Armenian men generally hid at home, and only women with covered heads were able to go out for shopping. For men it was dangerous to go out because they would be forcibly recruited to the army and then sent somewhere. The rumors were that once taken into the army, the Armenian men were killed.

Agop was young and did not listen to his older brother or to his mom. He looked young and was sure nobody would stop him. His brother bought him a document showing that he was a seventeen-year-old Turkish boy.

Agop was able to find a job as a young helper of a baker; he worked there for a year. Later he was a conductor of a train. He worked like this for almost two years.

One day in 1921, Agop was arrested by the military police. They found out that he was Armenian and took him forcibly to the army to do his military service for the country. He was twenty-three years old.

Was that same madness happening again? Maybe that's why his officer wanted him dead.

It was dark, and he continued walking carefully outside the forest and on the road till he touched something on the ground. He knew right away what it was. And then there was another dead body, and many others next to them. Tens of dead men had been left there as they were killed.

Agop felt the same strong shaking of his body again. He couldn't do anything but shake and shake, and now he knew what that shaking was. It was fear—fear for his life; fear for the lives of his brother, sister, and mother; fear of the unknown. What was going to happen to him? If they caught him, they would hang him twice—once for deserting from the army and once for being Armenian.

Slowly he overcame the fear and started looking at the faces of the bodies, looking for his brother. The moon came out so he could recognize the faces.

After a long time, he realized that his brother was not there.

Of course, he was not there. What was he thinking? Harry was in Istanbul. They should all be safe there.

Agop looked again at the bodies. These were not all the Armenian men living in Adapazar. There were many more Armenians in the city. Were they alive? There were no women here. Maybe the women were taken away and only the men were killed?

But where were the rest of the men? He had to find out the answers to all his questions.

"What's going on?" Agop asked loudly.

Agop knew what he had to do. He was still in a Turkish solder uniform, so he was not in immediate danger of being taken as an Armenian. He walked straight to the city and to the house of his best childhood friend, Mohamed, hoping that Mohamed would help him.

Mohamed's father, Ali, was a good friend to Agop's father before Sarkis passed away.

Agop remembered. After Harry moved his family to Istanbul, he rented a house for all of the nine members of the family.

Harry stayed in touch with Uncle Ali. Uncle Ali and his two sons, Mohamed and Kerim, went to Istanbul every two weeks to sell vegetables, fruits, eggs, butter, flour, honey, and other products they prepared. At night they slept at Harry's house. They sold them what they needed for food.

He remembered the nights after dinner when his brother Harry invited Ali and his two sons for a cup of coffee. They all were seated around the low table in the living room discussing the latest news.

Agop was praying that Ali and his family had not turned against the Armenians.

The city was not sleeping. There were solders everywhere, and other non-uniformed Turks were checking Armenian houses. Agop passed by them calmly. His hands and uniform were covered in blood, so nobody would think that he was not part of this operation.

When he got to Mohamed's house, the door was locked. He knocked and shouted loudly, "Open this door right away!"

At first, nobody answered, but then behind the door, an angry voice shouted back, "There are no Armenians here! Go away, or I will shoot you!"

"Open the door!" Agop shouted again. "I must talk with Mohamed!"

He heard low voices arguing, and then the door opened a bit and a big man holding a rifle in his hands looked at Agop.

"What do you want from Mohamed?" he demanded.

"It's me, Uncle Ali. Don't you recognize me? I'm Agop, Sarkis's son."

Ali looked at him, looked around carefully, and without saying a word pulled him in and closed the door.

They were the same people. They hadn't changed.

"Are you hurt?" Leila, Mohamed's mother, asked him while holding his hand. "Sit down, son. Are you okay?"

"What's going on here? Has everybody gone mad?" Agop asked with a breaking voice, his hands still shaking.

Leila was holding his hands trying to calm him down.

"You have to leave the city," she said. "It is not safe here for Armenians. Go to Istanbul. There you will be safer."

"What's going on?" Agop asked again.

"We do not know yet," Ali said, "but for sure some Armenian men were killed, others were arrested and are locked in the Armenian school, and all the rest are ordered to stay in their houses."

Ali looked at Agop and continued, "Every night bad things are happening with some of the Armenians, and we cannot help our good neighbors ..."

"Take my documents," said Kerim, Mohamed's younger brother. "Nobody will think that you are an Armenian. We are both almost the same size, and we both have green eyes. I'm seventeen years old, and they will not take you back to the army."

"Go now," said Ali. "Walk during the night, and hide somewhere during the day. If Allah wishes, in three or four nights, you will be in Istanbul."

Mohamed's mother gave him a bag with food and water and a clean pair of shoes, trousers, and shirt from Mohamed's closet. "You will need them when you get to Istanbul. God be with you!"

Ali gave him two golden coins and said, "Son, this will help you in the beginning. Go now and forgive us all."

Tears were flowing from Agop's eyes. He turned his head and walked back out of the room.

An hour later, Agop was outside the city walking to Istanbul.

❧

Vera was tired. She stopped talking, and Eric did not ask her any more questions. Instead, he said, "I think I'm going to go now. You are tired, and all these memories made you very emotional." Eric wanted to give her a break, but she did not let him stop her. She continued till her story was over.

They both stayed for a while not talking and just looking at each other. Then he stood up and walked slowly to his aunt. "I will come back again in a few days." He kissed her on the cheeks and left the house.

It was about noon, and the sun was strong in the skies over Plovdiv.

The stories were rich with many details Eric did not know, or maybe he forgot after they were told to him. Some of the details were different from what he remembered from the stories of his grandfather. After all he was only a boy when he was listening to his grandfather. Slowly he started remembering more details himself.

He decided to go to the Armenian graveyard, which was at the east end of Plovdiv beside the route to Istanbul.

Strange, he thought. *Even in their last bed in the grave, Armenians wanted to be close to the road going home. They were so much attached to their homeland! They missed it.*

Eric remembered his old grandfather, Agop, almost deaf. He was listening to a small transistor radio, placed right against his ear. It was playing Turkish music from a station in Istanbul. His eyes were closed, his head was shaking, and he was crying …

"Why are you crying, Grandpa?" Eric shook his arm and shouted in his ear.

"I have my memories, my son. I have my sweet and bitter memories." Agop smiled at him.

Eric walked slowly to the Armenian graveyard. He wanted to visit his parents and his grandparents. He wanted to talk with them and tell them how much he missed them.

The stories suddenly came back to his mind once more. This time he was sure he correctly remembered what he was told and how his grandfather came to Bulgaria. It was the story his aunt told him just half an hour ago.

❧

Four nights had passed, and Agop was now close to the big city. He washed his hands and face and put on clean clothes. Early the next morning, he was walking tall right in the middle of the road, headed to Istanbul.

It was about noon when he was almost in front of the big city that an officer stopped him and asked for his papers.

"What is your name, son?"

"Kerim, son of Ali. I'm from Adapazar."

"Why are you coming to Istanbul?"

"I want to work. I was helping an Armenian shoemaker, but he is dead now and the store is burned down. I have to work and help my family."

"How old are you?" the officer asked looking at his documents, where his age, size and color of his eyes were written.

"I'm seventeen," Agop answered.

"You look older," the officer said and looked closely at Agop's grown hairs on his face.

"I want to look older! Women like big men, not boys."

The officer smiled and gave him back the papers.

"Okay, son, go! Save money and help your family, because next year we will take you into the army. Turkey needs soldiers."

Agop smiled, wished the officer a good day, and started walking slowly into the big city.

The capital was crowded with so many different people. Men and women from foreign countries were walking in all directions and mixing with local people. He heard many languages: Turkish, Armenian, Greek, Bulgarian, German, Arabic, and Kurdish. This was a huge, old city, where different worlds and cultures were meeting and mixing together. He melted between them, became one of them.

Agop knew how to get to his aunt Claire's house. He had spent almost two years in Istanbul with his brother, sister, and mother, but they were living on the other side of the city—the one that was on European land.

He looked at the tramways and cars in the streets. Things had changed here, and there were new modern things he never saw before. Most amazing were the new cars. Beautiful cars with nicely dressed men and women were crossing the city. There were men dressed in European clothes—suits and big hats—and women with open faces and hair left free to be seen. They were dressed in long dresses and long gloves, wearing big light hats in different colors. This seemed to him so out of place and time.

These people did not know what was happening to the Armenians not far from Istanbul. He looked at the faces of the locals and did not see anything that would show that they knew what was going on.

The same thing will happen here. He started to shake again from fear. He had to leave the country with his family as soon as possible.

❧

An hour later, his aunt told him that a civilian man came earlier the same day to ask for him.

"He said that if we help you, they will arrest us for helping an army deserter. You cannot stay here! Run! Go to the seaport and try to take a boat to Bulgaria!

"Your brother took your mom, and together with Nicole and her husband, they went to Plovdiv in Bulgaria. They took the train about two months ago. This train went to Munich through Plovdiv. Harry took special passes from the Germans so they could leave Turkey.

"You cannot take the train. The military police check everybody at the railway station. Try to catch a boat to Burgas on the Bulgarian coast. Once in Bulgaria, go to Plovdiv. Your family is there.

"Go find them! If you stay here, they will arrest you, and you are finished."

She gave him a few silver coins and said, "It's not much but will help you buy food and shelter for few days. Take tramway #5; it will take you to the port. No, do not take the main entrance out of the house. Go out from the back door. Right away—now!"

On the way out, Agop remembered what had happened and said, "Aunt, Armenian men in Adapazar are being killed, and women and children are being taken away. These crazy men might come here also. You have to run out from Turkey. Armenians will not be safe even here."

He ran out of the house, and without turning his head, he walked slowly away on the street and turned the corner, never looking back. Then he took tramway #5 going to the port. He did not know where he was going. It was enough to know that the tram was going to the port and to his freedom.

Was he dreaming? He saw his Turkish officer with a few solders coming up on the same train. They were looking for him. He slowly moved to the end of the tram and turned his back to them, praying the tram would stop before they saw him. As soon as the tram stopped, he jumped out, mixing with the people waiting at the station. Without turning, he took the way to the port, his last hope to catch a boat to Burgas.

Finally he was at the seaport. There were many boats—small, not so small, big, and very big ones.

"Now what?" he asked himself. "How am I going to find a boat going to Bulgaria?

"What are the chances that this boat will be going to Burgas?

"Where do I buy a ticket? How much will it cost?

"Are they going to ask me why I'm going there?

"Oh my God, when will this nightmare end?"

He started shaking again. There were too many unknowns, and behind each corner and man, he could see people watching him and waiting for him just to ask a wrong question; then they would find out who he was.

He was an Armenian, an army deserter. There was no chance for him to escape! They would find him here at the port, and they would hang him.

"Calm down!" Agop said to himself, and oddly enough, he calmed down right away.

"Think! Fear will not help you. Do not let it shake you again!"

I can do that. I'm not afraid of anything! I can do it!

"What would my father do if he were here?" Agop asked himself.

First he would find out if any boat was going to Bulgaria. He would go to that small pub facing the port and sit there and watch first without saying anything.

"You have to watch, listen, and think!" It was almost as if he saw his father advising him.

Agop went to the pub and sat down next to other people who were talking loudly and drinking wine. He stayed there for a few hours came to know most of the guys.

Some were local guys waiting in the pub for somebody to hire them for any job at the port.

Others were fishermen just relaxing after a long day.

There were a few sailors from different boats. Agop ordered a new cup of the sweet wine and moved closer to the table of the sailors, trying to catch their words. Finally he heard one of them saying that his boat was leaving for Burgas early in the morning, and he promised his friends that he would continue drinking and not get drunk till it was time to leave. This was a big guy, with huge hands and a mustache.

They were all drunk, and everybody was talking without listening to what the others were saying. Agop realized that he had to pretend to be drunk also, so as not to draw attention of spies who might be looking for deserters like him.

He ordered wine for the men at the table and moved next to them, saying that he wanted to be a sailor like them and cross the seas and see different places and a lot of women. They started laughing, and soon he became one of them.

Finally the time came, and his friend had to go to the boat. Agop stood up also, and they walked out together to the port.

"I want to come with you to Bulgaria. I heard the women there are beautiful and easy," Agop said.

The sailor smiled and said, "Come on. I will hide you, and then the captain will not throw you in the sea. I will make you a great sailor like me, and you will cross the world.

"Here is the boat. Now wait for me to go up, because there is an officer checking in the people. Can you swim?"

"Yes. Why?" Agop asked.

"Go in the water, around the boat, and wait close to the nose till I throw you a rope."

Soon after that, Agop was onboard. The boat left the quay and went to open sea.

Agop was tired. His friend was sleeping, but he was afraid what would happen next. His nightmare did not have an end yet.

How was he going to hide in the boat? How was he going to leave it? How was he going to enter Burgas without being arrested and sent back to Istanbul? *I must not sleep, or I will risk being caught*, he thought.

Agop felt so tired. It was his fourth or fifth night without normal sleep—or maybe he was sleeping?

He woke up from loud voices and heavy cursing of sailors, whose time had come to report for their shift. His friend was shaking him.

"Come up with me, or you will miss the chance to go to Burgas. We are arriving … put on this sailor shirt and this cap, boy. Keep your head down!" His friend put a sailor cap on Agop's head.

"I will help you leave the boat." He looked at Agop, and then continued in a low voice, "Next time do not scream in Armenian if you do not want to get arrested."

"What are you talking about?" Agop pretended angrily that he did not understand.

"Let's go now. Do you have money with you? You have to bribe a few guys on the Bulgarian side to let you in."

Soon they all came out of the boat and had to go through check-in. A Bulgarian officer was there waiting for their papers to give them permission to enter the country.

"Go to him!" his friend said. "Give him all the money you have, and pray he will not arrest you right away."

"Thank you, Mustafa, I will never forget your help."

Agop prepared a golden coin in his hand and went straight to the officer.

He said to him in Turkish, "I'm an Armenian. Please help me enter; if not, I will be killed. All the Armenian men are being killed, and women and children are being deported somewhere.

"Please help me …" And he put his hand with the coin in the officer's hand.

"Go in," the officer said. "Welcome to Bulgaria!"

And Agop was now in Bulgaria.

Without realizing it, Eric had come to the entrance of the Armenian graveyard.

A gypsy woman was selling flowers at the door. He bought two bouquets of red roses and entered the graveyard. He found the tombs of his parents and grandparents.

He read the names on one of them: his mother, Nelly, his father, Santo, and his grandfather, Agop.

On the other one were the names of his grandmother, Arakssi, and his great-grandmother, Ovsana.

His grandfather had lived for eighty-seven years; his grandmother had lived for eighty-five years.

His father lived only sixty-eight years, and his mom seventy-five years.

His great-grandmother, Ovsana, lived only forty-nine years.

Eric was praying for their souls to be together and happy …

He stayed in front of their tombs without thinking of anything—just letting himself be there. Somehow he felt much better, as if he had met and spoken with his parents.

"I will be back," Eric said and left.

He felt even better when he came out of the Armenian graveyard.

He was on vacation, and he intended to have fun and relax.

His family was waiting for him at his sister's home, and he rushed to join them for a late lunch.

The next morning, Renee went to see her aunt in Plovdiv.

At the same time, Eric took the bus to Sofia and then a taxi to his uncle Ed's apartment. It was tradition to meet every year when he was on vacation. They both looked forward to seeing each other.

Uncle Ed was more than just an uncle for Eric. He was like a father, and he knew Ed loved him too as his son.

Uncle Ed had cooked an Armenian soup, topics, which his grandmother Arakssi used to make for them when they were kids. They all loved it, and Uncle Ed had prepared it for him, surprisingly well. Then they had green beans, also done according to a recipe of Mezmama's. At the end was the big surprise: anushabour, an Armenian dessert—wheat pudding with dried grapes and walnuts, which today everybody in Bulgaria knows by the Armenian name.

"Uncle Ed, that was really good. Bravo! Thank you for the food. Everything was so good and delicious. You know, you are a good cook!"

"Wait, I have some peaches as well and watermelon and Bulgarian cherries," his uncle offered.

"Oh my God! There is no room anymore, but I love Bulgarian fruits. They are so sweet!"

After this great lunch, they went to the living room and continued talking about Eric's children, Nevena and Maya. They spoke about the marriage of Nevena and Antony, about Antony and his parents, Rumina and Krassimir, and about the little Krassi. They spoke about his wife Renee and her parents, Nikola and Nina, who were living now in Ottawa in an apartment not far from their house.

"I am so happy we were able to bring Renee's parents to Ottawa. This was very good not only for them and us, but also for our children. Our children were able to enjoy the love of their grandparents in a foreign country," Eric said. "It was not easy, and even now is not easy, but we are happy to have them in Ottawa."

"How is Nikola doing? I heard he has cancer."

"Yes, unfortunately he has cancer of the esophagus. It has been growing for the last two years, and now it is not allowing him to pass his food down to the stomach. He is eating only soups and liquids. Except for that, he is doing well, and his morale is high.

"Both Nikola and Nina walk twice a day. I admire how active and full of life they are. It is a pleasure to talk to them and see them. We see each other almost every day," Eric said, and then he changed the topic.

"How is my cousin Alexa doing after the operation?" he asked.

"She is much better now. They are both with Dinko in Balchik at their apartment on the seacoast."

"I hope I can see them when we go to Sunny Beach," Eric said. "How are Boris, Christy, and little Dana doing?" he asked.

"They are very good," Uncle Ed said and showed him pictures of his great-granddaughter Dana, with her grandmother, Alexa. Then he showed him a picture of Dana with her parents, Boris and Christina, holding their daughter in their hands.

"So, Dana and Krassi were born with only fifteen days' difference. I hope they will stay as close as we did with Alexa." Eric smiled and continued, "They will be second cousins, as I am with Dave. It's funny I thought about this," he added.

Uncle Ed looked at him, put down the pictures, and as if the moment had come, asked him, "Okay, tell me now, what happened? Did you finish your arguments? Was it done in an intelligent way?"

"Yes, it is over now. But it ended just a few days before we went on vacation. It was very difficult for both of us to keep our calm and complete our arguments without really fighting and without breaking up our relationship." Eric crossed his hands in front of his chest.

He looked down and said, "I'm still upset about many things, but I know in a few weeks, I will be feeling much better. I'm sure Dave feels the same way. The last year and a half were very difficult, I'm sure, for him also.

"I need some time to be able to calm down and then look back on our last twenty years. As Dave told me recently, we worked together longer than he worked with his father, Avedis."

"Have you signed all the documents in front of the lawyers?" Edwin asked.

"Yes, everything is signed. Now we are no longer partners but just cousins, and time will show if we will still be friends."

Eric continued talking. "I need time to go over everything from the beginning and put together the good and the bad, and I hope the good will be much heavier than the bad.

"You know, Uncle Ed, I came to realize that most ordinary people can forget all the good just for one bad thing. Like a drop of black paint in a pot of white paint. The paint is no longer white ..." He stopped for a moment and then said:

"Uncle Ed, I told you I want to write a book about my grandparents' emigration and about our lives and the new emigration we had to face in new times."

"So, you want Dave to read this book, don't you?"

"Uncle, we had a difficult, stressful life. This has nothing to do with Dave. Actually, he helped us. It is mostly due to the emigration. I was afraid of losing my partnership and work because I might not be able to do my job. I was afraid I would not be able to provide for my family during our emigration ..."

"You did not have an emigration," his uncle stated flatly.

Eric looked at him and thought to himself:

My God! He doesn't know anything about the struggles of modern-time emigrants. Only an emigrant knows what it is. Only an emigrant can understand it with just a few words. The rest will need much more time … This is one more reason to write the book.

"You do not understand, Uncle Ed. I couldn't speak loudly what was on my heart, what were our feelings, what we went through—all of us: Renee, me, and the kids."

While Eric was talking, a message came on his phone from Maya: "I need to come to Ottawa for a while. Here I have no friends and no relatives. I need your advice."

It was a message from his daughter. Eric looked at his watch. With the time difference of ten hours, it was now early in the morning, about seven thirty, in Victoria.

"I'm sorry, Uncle Ed; I need to write Maya a message."

"What's happening?"

"Well, she broke up with her boyfriend. She has been living with him for the last year in an apartment in downtown Victoria. She is emotionally hurt, so she needs our support."

"Tell her to wait for you to come back to Ottawa. This will give her time to calm down and realize which is better: for her to stay in Victoria, or come back to Ottawa."

Eric wrote her a message:

"Please wait for us to come back and then decide what to do."

Then he called Renee in Plovdiv to tell her about Maya.

"Yes, we just spoke on Skype," Renee told him. "She doesn't know what she will do yet. It's a weekend and she feels alone, but tomorrow she will go to work and for sure she will feel better. Let's wait till Monday, and then we will talk with her again."

Eric closed the phone and looked at his uncle.

"You worry too much about Maya," his uncle said. "She is a big girl."

"Yes, I know, but she is alone there in a big city among foreigners, without friends. I'm afraid that something bad might happen to her that she will need our help, but we are so far away—six hours' flight by plane ..."

"Eric, you told me you were happy when she decided to go to Victoria," his uncle reminded him.

"Yes, I still am, because there are good opportunities for her business-wise, but we are all sad and we miss her."

"How about Nevena? She doesn't live with you either?" Uncle Ed asked him.

"Nevena is ten minutes away from us, and we see each other at least once every week. She is not alone. She has her husband, Antony, and many friends she grew up with in Ottawa. She can come and see us or her grandparents anytime she needs something.

"Often we invite Nevena and Antony for lunch or dinner at home, and we enjoy each other's company. Now with the baby Krassi around, this will be even more enjoyable and more often," Eric answered.

"Do not worry about Maya. She will be fine. She is young, and she will make new friends and not be alone. Do not scare her, but keep on giving her courage to continue her efforts to grow her business in Victoria. If she decides to come back, support her decision, but do not try to influence her to come back. Let her decide on her own."

"Thank you, Uncle Ed. I feel better now. After all, she is not so far—only six hours by plane, plus we see each other on Skype, which is amazing." Eric smiled and continued, "I remember twenty years ago when we went to Ottawa. We needed to talk with our parents so much, we were calling them every weekend. At the time, this was very, very expensive. We were spending $100 per month for overseas conversations. The money was not enough for all our needs, but it was enough for our conversations.

"I was wondering at the time how a hundred years ago, emigrants were surviving without the telephone. They were writing letters to each other and waiting months for the answers."

"This was a real emigration," his uncle said. "They had to cross the ocean by boat, and this took them several weeks. Many got sick and died during the crossing.

Today it takes just a day to arrive in the new world, and if you miss the old Europe, you just save some money and come back again on vacation."

"It is not so easy to be an emigrant today, Uncle Ed—not as easy as you make it sound." Eric bit his lips and then continued:

"Yes, certain things are easier, because of technology and progress, but the human side of the emigration is still difficult. It takes a lot of guts and dedication to stay in the new world as an emigrant, instead of just catching the first plane back home and enjoying what we missed—parents, home, comfort, friends, native language, no pressure to do something right away, and many, many other simple things we took for granted back home."

Eric was shaking his head, filled with emotions. "We all had to accept working in places we did not like, jobs we did not choose, but we accepted them—and the managers who took advantage of us. We did not know how to speak well, we did not know our rights, and we were afraid to lose our jobs.

"These emigrants had to work long hours every day, often running after finishing one job during the day to a second job during the night in restaurants, delivering pizzas, or working in sweatshops in manufacturing. They were postponing going to school and learning the language, even though the Canadian government was giving six or more months paid for adaptation and education."

Eric stopped for a moment to take his breath and try to calm down, realizing that he was talking too fast and too emotionally.

"Uncle, we are an example. My wife, Renee, went on this program for about six months to learn French and English and adapt to the life in Canada. It's a great program, where they teach you languages—words and grammar, how to write and how to read. They also teach you your rights, places to go and enjoy, how to find work, how to read books from the library, and many other useful things. It is just a wonderful way to adapt to the country," Eric said.

He took a breath and continued, "I was hoping one day to be able to do that myself. Here I am twenty years after we first arrived, and I never took that chance. I was putting all my active hours and energy in the work ten to twelve hours every day during the week, four to five hours every Saturday, sometimes even on Sundays to catch up with my work.

"The first three years, after work I did go to French courses in a nearby school three times a week from 7:00 p.m. to 10:00 p.m. I also went to English courses twice a week in a college, again from 7:00 p.m. to 10:00 p.m. On Saturdays I took courses to catch up with my computer knowledge. I learned Excel, AutoCAD, Word, and simple accounting. I did not have the luxury to stop working and concentrate on education in Ottawa. Even though I graduated from the university in Bulgaria, it was not enough for me to do my job properly without learning some basics, such as language and certain technical requirements." Eric went on.

"Maybe you can do it now?" his uncle interrupted him, smiling. It was clear he was getting tired. "Now you have all the time you want. Now you are retired, and you can spend time for things you want," he added, speaking slowly.

"Actually, you are right. This is a good idea. I still need to improve my English and learn better French. I will give it a second thought," Eric said, realizing that he had spoken for too long. His uncle was getting tired, and Eric needed to give him a break.

But before Eric suggested stopping and getting ready for sleep, Edwin said as if talking to himself, "I wouldn't go to a foreign country as an emigrant. No, I would not …"

"Let's go to sleep, uncle. It's getting late. I'm tired also. Tomorrow we will continue."

Eric went to his bed in the living room, where his uncle had prepared sheets and blankets for him. He couldn't sleep. He felt bad that he spoke so emotionally; maybe he intimidated his uncle. It was not right doing that, and he did not want to make his uncle feel that he did not respect him. On the contrary, he had always admired him. He learned many things from him, and his uncle had always been an example for him for achieving great results.

His grandmother, Arakssi, always gave him as an example for her grandkids. She would say, "Look how far he went. He became vice president of a big corporation. He was always studying and working very hard. Nobody helped him, only himself and us, his family. He was also an Armenian by origin, but he succeeded in Bulgaria. Learn from him!"

Eric recognized that his uncle Edwin did become one of the most important key people in a huge and very profitable corporation in Bulgaria. He was vice president of product development and at the same time director of the research institute. The corporation had twenty-seven factories all over Bulgaria, and they had very modern technology and machinery. Their market was Eastern Europe, Russia, and the Middle East.

Eric had his eyes closed, but pictures and words were coming to him and keeping him awake. He again heard the voice of his uncle:

"Eric, why are you writing a book about your grandfather? Write a book about your father. He is the one who really deserves your attention. If it were not for him, my father couldn't have survived his illness. Your father was taking care of my parents, and he was supporting me to finish my education at the university.

"Eric, your father, Santo, was a great man. He was there for all of us. His life was a whole life of family dedication. He was a strong person, and when at the end he was very sick, he did not want anybody to come to see him. He did not complain, and he did not talk about his problems.

"He missed you a lot when you decided to go to Canada, but he never tried to stop you and he was hoping you would do well in Canada. Your sister Lisa and her husband, Arak, took good care of your parents. You should remember this."

"I will, Dad, I will, and I will write for everybody because I love them all." Eric was now talking to his father, whom he missed, and slowly falling asleep.

Just before completely falling asleep, he remembered again the vision he had the first night they arrived in Ottawa. It was of an old man with a long white beard and strange long clothes, from his head clear down to his feet. The old man said to him:

"Eric, you will succeed. You will learn to fly. You will help a lot of people, but you will not be able to help your father … You will miss him …"

September 2011
Ottawa

Three months had passed since Eric retired, or as he preferred to say, semiretired.

Everybody in Ottawa, in addition to his close family, was expecting that he would go back to work. He would do something. There was social pressure that he was still young and it is not normal not to work.

He met with his consultant accountant, who told him that the best thing was to invest his money in real estate—a block of apartments. He advised Eric to take a loan from a bank and buy an old building with at least twenty apartments.

Eric felt a bit upset that the accountant was insisting that he was still young and had to do something. At the same time, Eric was embarrassed to say that he was perfectly happy not actively working, that he was busy with other things.

Eric felt as if he were doing something wrong.

He thought to himself: *I have worked under pressure and stress since I came to Canada twenty years ago, with an average of sixty to sixty-five hours per week working. Isn't that equal to thirty to thirty-two years with the standard forty hours per week? I feel tired and do not want to take new loans from a bank and start over again. I feel like I'm at least sixty-five, even though I'm actually just fifty-seven. Perhaps in a few years, I will feel different, and I will again grow a desire to do something new …*

I spoke with Renee about it, and we both agreed that we must not risk investing again in a business.

Neither of us is ready to take out new loans and jump in the system again. It's a perfectly well-designed system that makes you work again and again, always running after the money.

It is hard to stop and very hard to get out of it.

Eric was thinking about the changes in their lives since he semiretired.

He invested the money from selling his shares to Dave in the stock market. With most of it, he bought guaranteed investment certificates (GICs) with different maturities (like one, two, three, four, five, and even more years)—enough to provide for a modest income and carry them to sixty-five to sixty-seven years of age.

I started learning about managing investments in the stock market. My approach is conservative. I have chosen a very conservative portfolio, which was designed to fight against inflation, but not really make the money grow, as financial advisors always try to tell us. Maybe they are right, but I cannot trust them with our money, which we got with so much hard work.

We are not greedy, and we also know that the average life span in Canada is eighty years. We will be lucky if we make it till eighty. As for our kids, the best heritage that we could give them is our example.

"Be honest, study, and work hard. Be responsible!"

Also, our house is mortgage-free, and it will go to our kids after we are gone.

Suddenly Eric remembered his Grandmother Arakssi. When she was old, sick, and very close to her end, she told him:

"Eric, I do not have much left to live, and I'm not afraid to die. I'm just afraid I will miss my grandchildren and great-grandchildren. I do not have anything to give them. I have given them everything I had—my love. I have seventy-five dollars left from my pension. Please divide it equally among all of them. Let them buy chocolates. I hope they will remember me ..."

Eric remembered his grandmother well. He loved her so much, and he also missed her.

I'm writing this book for you, Grandma, so we all— your grandchildren and great-grandchildren—remember you.

And so now I'll again get busy with writing the book.

&

Grandmother Arakssi was six years old when she went to Bulgaria in 1912 with her mother, Ovsana Kaladian, and her little three-year-old brother, Hagop.

I remember her stories, and I also spoke with my sister Lisa, my cousin Alexa, my uncle Ed, and my aunt Vera, to find out what they remembered.

Ovsana and her two children were born in Yozgat, in central Anatolia in Turkey.

In the early spring of 1912, Ovsana's husband, Haroutun, died after a few months being sick. She became a young widow.

She was only twenty years old and already had two small children. Her two parents were living with her younger brother and sister. Her elder brother was twenty-two years old, and he was helping her husband in the shop. After her husband passed away, it was her older brother who took care of her and the children.

According to my cousin Alexa, they all moved to Istanbul, where her elder brother had friends and started work as a carpenter.

I do not remember clearly if they moved to Istanbul, but this was very possible because it was much easier to find work there and there was a large Armenian community. For a young widow with two small children, this was probably the best decision. This also better explains the political contacts her elder brother made with Antranik Pasha and his followers—fighters for Armenian independence.

Ovsana was blessed with a talent. She was able to speak well, and more importantly, feel the problems and worries of other people. Women came to see her and asked her to look in their coffee cups and tell them about their lives, giving them some kind of clue about the future and what to do. She never took money for this, but now that she was left with no husband, she accepted the food and clothes they offered her.

She had the same dream every night after losing her husband. In her dream, an old man with a long white beard was telling her to take her family and go to Jerusalem.

After discussing it with her brother, they decided to go. Every year, with the permission and protection of the Turkish government, the Armenian Church in Istanbul organized a pilgrimage to the Holy City of Jerusalem, where there was a large Armenian church. Ovsana, with her brother and two children, prepared for the long trip.

After a few months of traveling and stopping for rest in many small villages and cities with Armenian populations, they finally arrived in Jerusalem. They had almost no food left, and their hope was that the church would help them find a job and shelter somewhere in the city.

What were they going to do? Ovsana prayed every day to God to help them, to show them what to do and where to go next.

She had a big responsibility taking care of two small children.

Her brother was another thing. He had different dreams, and this was a problem for her. She was afraid of losing him. He was the only man left around her, and he protected her and the children.

His thoughts ran toward something else, very dangerous. When they came to Jerusalem, he told her that he wanted to join the Armenian freedom movement. He wanted to fight for Armenian independence.

She had felt his desire for many days before he decided to tell her about it.

They both started working at the Christian hospital in Jerusalem, where the Armenian priest had influence. The priest also helped them find an Armenian house, and they moved in. An older Armenian family was happy to accommodate them.

Ovsana left the children at home with the old Armenian couple and went to work every day as a sanitarian. Her brother also was working, doing whatever was needed. He was a carpenter, and he was good with his hands. Every night after work, he stayed late, meeting with other Armenian men.

One night he came to her room and woke her up.

"Ovsana, I'm going. I'm sorry, but I cannot stay here and do nothing when others are risking their lives for Armenia." His voice was low, coming deep from his chest and with no hesitation, leaving no room for her to try to stop him.

"You will be safer here in Jerusalem. I do not think the Turks will go openly against the peaceful Christian population here in the heart of the Holy City.

"Soon there will be a big war. Bulgarians, Greeks, Serbians, and Montenegrins are getting ready to start a war against the Ottoman Empire for the complete liberation of their lands and people. We Armenians back home in Turkey should join them and fight for our lives, faith, and independence." He looked straight into her eyes.

"My brothers are leaving tomorrow morning, and I'm going with them. We are going to join the Armenian Battalion of Antranik Pasha." He turned to the children and kissed them on the cheeks while they were sleeping.

"Garabed, I cannot stay here, far away from you. Where are you going?" Ovsana asked him.

"I cannot tell you that."

"We are going to die here without you," Ovsana cried. "Who will protect us? Tell me where we should go so we can stay close to you." Ovsana's voice was shaking.

"You are our only family left," Ovsana said.

"I promise I will tell you. When we arrive, I will send somebody with a letter for you; I will tell you where you can go to follow me."

He stood up, kissed her and the sleeping children good-bye, and walked out without looking back.

Ovsana felt alone. She was scared and sad. She closed her eyes and started praying to God. There were so many things to pray for.

She prayed for her children, for herself, for her big brother, and for her parents and younger brother and sister left back in Turkey to be healthy and alive. She prayed for God to give her strength and show her how to keep her children safe. She prayed to God to help her stay close to her elder brother, who was her protector. She was hoping to come out of Turkey and be able to save her children and provide them with everything they would need.

As the days passed, Ovsana continued going to work every day. She waited for a letter from her brother.

Three weeks later, a man came to her house and gave her a letter and some money from her brother. In the letter, Garabed asked her to trust the man, who was going to take them to Cairo in Egypt and help them find a house in the Armenian neighborhood.

The man was waiting for her outside the house. Ovsana did not hesitate any longer. She thanked the old Armenian couple for their help. She took her two children and the few belongings they had, and she left with this stranger and with the strong belief in God.

In a few weeks, they arrived in Cairo. The man found them an Armenian house and left them there. He told her to wait for her brother to send her a new letter where to go next.

Almost a month passed without any news from Garabed. Finally another man came with a letter to her. This letter was pretty much the same as the first one. This time the man was an Egyptian merchant who spoke perfect Turkish, who was going to Bulgaria and was going to take them to Shumen.

There was no other explanation or words about what was happening to Garabed.

A few days later, they went to Alexandria, and from there a week later, they took a boat to Varna, Bulgaria.

It was early October 1912 when Ovsana, with her two children, arrived at the Armenian church in Shumen. This was an old Armenian church, St. Mary, built in 1834 on a hill with a beautiful view to the old city of Shumen. On the other side was another hill, with the ruins of an old Bulgarian fortress from the early eighth century. Big trees surrounded the church, as if they were protecting the church and the Armenians living nearby.

She was desperate for news of her brother. She did not know what was going on. She hoped that finally she could see her brother. The Egyptian man told her that his job was done, and now she had to see the priest. He was going to tell her where her brother was and where she was going to stay.

Ovsana was tired. She and her two children had been traveling for four months, crossing the Ottoman Empire from one end to the other. Now they were in Bulgaria, and she was on the edge of her forces. She looked at the children and prayed to God, thanking Him that He had saved them. They were skinny, but in good health.

The priest met her with a smile and gave them his blessings. He told Ovsana that her brother was alive and was actually a volunteer together with 269 other Armenians.

Antranik Pasha, or as the Bulgarians here were calling him, General Antranik, had formed a battalion of Armenian soldiers. They had joined the Bulgarian Army within the Macedonian-Adrianopolitan Volunteer Corps. Their training base was between Shumen and Varna, but since the war against Turkey started a day ago, they had left for the front, and now they were fighting for the full liberation of Bulgaria and for Armenian independence as well.

Ovsana was about to faint. She was shaking, and tears ran down both sides of her face.

"Do not be afraid, my child!" the priest said. "God is protecting you. I can see that. You came out from the Ottoman Empire just before the war started. Only God knows what will happen now to all the Armenians back home in our lands under Turkish rule.

"Let's pray for your brother and for all the other Armenian volunteers, who right now are fighting for us." The priest made a cross sign with his right hand, and then he took in his arms the little Arakssi, She started playing with his silver cross, hanging on his neck.

"I see you've been in Jerusalem, you little princess," the priest said, touching Arakssi's hand where there was a tattoo of Jesus's head. Then he picked up her other hand, where another tattoo of a cross was visible inside her wrist.

"Ovsana, your brother brought you here to Bulgaria to save you. Here you and your children will be safe and free. The Bulgarian constitution gives equal rights to all minorities, including all the Armenians living in Bulgaria.

"I'm going to help you find Armenian families that will be glad to take you home and help you rest and recover from the long journey you have taken.

"Come every day to the church for news. Let's pray for your brother and the others to come back alive." The priest

---

gave them his blessings and asked them to wait for him till he got free.

Five months passed, and every day Ovsana came back to the church to pray for her brother and to hear the news from the front. There were many other Armenians, whose brothers, sons, or husbands were at the front, fighting for independence and freedom.

One day in April 1913 an officer from the Bulgarian Army was in the church when she arrived. He spoke about the victories of the Bulgarian Army against the Turkish Army. Unfortunately, many brave men—Bulgarians and Armenians—had given their lives for the full liberation of the Bulgarian people and territories. He said that these men would never be forgotten by a grateful Bulgaria.

Tsar Ferdinand was giving Bulgarian citizenship to all the Armenian relatives who had lost husbands, brothers, sons, or grandsons in the war.

Then the priest started reading the names of all the Armenian solders from the Armenian Battalion. It was a long list. Almost all of them were dead or missing. Ovsana heard the name of her brother, who was missing and most probably dead.

She was now left completely alone with her two small children. She was free in a foreign country—Bulgaria.

When the priest came to her later on and tried to calm her down, she was still in shock.

"Ovsana, you can be proud of your brother. He came here as a volunteer to fight for the Armenians, and he will not be forgotten. Armenians in Bulgaria will be remembered and honored because of men like him. God be with him!"

Ovsana was there listening to him. She suddenly stopped crying. "No, he is not dead … I feel it, and I know it. He is alive," Ovsana said with a firm voice. Now she was calm, but her eyes were seeing something far away, something only she could see.

The priest looked at her and smiled with his eyes. "We will pray for him and the other missing to be alive. You never know—miracles are happening.

"If I have any news, I will send you a letter, but now you have to start thinking about yourself and your children. You have to adapt to your new life here in Bulgaria.

"You must learn Bulgarian. Find a job. Put the kids in Armenian school so they do not forget that they are Armenians. Help them get a good education in Bulgarian so they can integrate well here. You are young, and you should get married."

The priest told her that he would write a letter to the Armenian church in Plovdiv, where there was a large Armenian community.

"I will ask them to help you settle there. Take the letter with you. You will find friends, shelter, work, and a future for yourself and your children. The priest will help you give a good education to your kids. God be with you, my child!"

❧

It was strange. Now that Eric was writing about his Grandmother Arakssi and his great-grandmother Ovsana, he realized something important.

It was about his great-uncle, whose real name he had forgotten. Nobody remembered his real name, and Eric just decided to call him Garabed. He did not remember his family name either. Too bad! Was it Kaladian, or was this the family name of Ovsana's husband? Eric didn't know.

Maybe I can find it in the archives of the Bulgarian Army. Or maybe somebody will remember it. After all, how many boys from Yozgat were there in the Antranik Pasha Armenian Volunteer Battalion during the Balkan War of 1912? There were just 270 Armenian soldiers, and one of them was my great-granduncle. Maybe the archives in the Armenian church in Shumen will have the list of the 270 Armenian soldiers.

If he had not guided Ovsana and her two children out of the Ottoman Empire, most likely they would have died.

❧

On October 8, 1912, the Balkan War started. In May 1913, Turkey lost the war against Bulgaria, Greece, Serbia, and Montenegro. The war continued throughout 1913, but this time between the allies. Serbia, Greece, Montenegro and Romania attacked Bulgaria for who will take the biggest shares of the liberated territories. The First World War started in 1914 and continued till 1918.

The Armenian genocide started in Turkey on April 24, 1915, and continued till 1922. Almost 1.5 million Armenians were killed or left to die during deportations.

These were very difficult years for Ovsana. She remained in Plovdiv, Bulgaria. She never married again. She worked hard, struggling for the future of her children.

Arakssi and Hagop graduated from the Armenian school in Plovdiv and learned both Bulgarian and Armenian. They learned as well Turkish in school and from her mother who was speaking Turkish and Armenian fluently.

In 1923, Arakssi met Agop, Eric's grandfather, and they got married. She was seventeen years old; her mother, Ovsana, was only thirty-two years old, but already had gray hair.

Eric's Grandmother Arakssi had the same talent as her mother. She was very good at telling stories.

Her grandchildren loved listening to her. She talked or read books in Armenian or Bulgarian, and she sang both Armenian and Bulgarian songs.

She prayed for her grandchildren to become good people and to succeed in life.

She threw water behind her children and grandchildren for good luck when they were going for exams in school and later at the university. They always took excellent notes, so they always did well on the exams.

Secretly—hiding it from her husband—she looked in the empty coffee cups and told them about their good future and how to achieve it. It was all written there in their coffee cups, and they believed her and tried to follow her advice.

We all miss her … and remember her, Eric thought.

November 2011
Ottawa

Eric decided to send the story he had written so far to his uncle and ask him for his comments.

He waited a few days, but his uncle did not send him back any e-mail. He started wondering if his uncle was getting upset about something he wrote.

Eric sent an e-mail to his cousin Alexa with a copy of the story and also asked her to find out why his uncle was not saying anything.

On the next day, he got Alexa's answer.

He opened the e-mail from her.

> *Eric, it is very good! I like it very much!*
>
> *Is it true that my grandmother said that she left her love to us? Why didn't anybody tell me this?*
>
> *This is the best thing she could leave to me. Thank you for that …*
>
> *As I read your story, I remembered so many good things from our childhood.*

Did you know that I wrote some short stories about our childhood? Every time I felt bad, I looked for the safety of my childhood memories, and the best way for me was to sit down and right away put it down in writing.

I have not shared this with anybody yet, but now when I see your writing, I feel less embarrassed to share my feelings and writing with you and other members of our family.

Do you want to read one of them? I know it is naïve and sentimental, and I hope you will not laugh at me.

As for my father, do not worry! He is not upset with you. It's just that his back is hurting and he is avoiding staying in front of the computer. I'm sure he will read your book and send you his comments. The only thing is that he will be more critical than me. You know him well.

Kisses to everybody,

With love,
Alexa

P.S. Please see attached my first short story ... ☺

Eric opened the attached file and started reading.

Spring at the Childhood House

She is wonderful! This is the season when the house is the most beautiful.

As we know, the plum is the first tree to bloom in the backyard. The whole tree is covered with white flowers. His branches softly knock on Eric's and Alexa's windows and enter in the little balcony of Mezmama and Mezhairig's room.

When you go farther into the yard, you can see a big mulberry tree, with brown bark. He spreads his big branches almost over the entire yard. His leaves are so green and sparkling. You can smell the aroma of flowers and green trees everywhere.

Next to the back wall, you can see the gentle flowers of the quince tree. On his left side is the lilac, with heavy dark lilac-colored blooms. How wonderful is the sweet aroma carried on the soft wind!

From here starts Mezmama Arakssi's garden. There are two rows of flowers separated with a row of stone tiles. Here during the summer, roses, fuchsias, flames, and marigolds all bloom.

The aquiline flowers cover almost the entire window of the small shaded area of the yard, where the wood and coal for the winter fire are stored. His pale lilac blooms go up on the roof and spread the pleasant smell throughout the yard.

In the middle of the yard, between the quince and the mulberry trees, is a smaller garden—it belongs to Mezmama as well.

Here are the best hortenzia flowers on the street. Their blooms, as big as the balls with which the kids play, are gentle rose in color.

The entire ground of this smaller garden is covered with big gray stone tiles. These are smooth, hot, flat, heavy stones that make the yard look even bigger and more inviting.

The sun is shining over the house and the yard, but under the big trees there are thick shadows, which throw a magic spell.

Suddenly a clatter of running naughty small feet breaks the silence.

Alexa and Eric are running down the wooden ladder, and their joyful cries are carried over the yard.

On this wonderful fresh spring morning, both kids were racing to reach the kitchen, where Mezmama was waiting for them with French toast, cheese, and milk with cacao.

They started to eat quickly, talking at the same time, explaining to Grandma what their plans were for today.

Mezmama was listening to them and smiling. She told them to stay in the yard so she would not worry about them.

When they were small, every day Mezmama told them children's stories.

They cried with the sad stories of the poor little girl who was selling matches to survive. They were happy with the wild swans' transformation into princes. In this way, day after day, the magic world of the children's stories taught them to be good and sensitive and to believe in the power of good.

Already five years old, they asked Mezmama to tell them a story.

Mezmama could not refuse, and soon the story began.

The small kitchen became silent, and only Mezmama's voice was carried in the air. She was talking about the magic world of a prince and a princess.

Alexa and Eric were slowly opening their small mouths to be able to take the next bite and sip from the milk without losing sight of their grandma's mouth.

She was seated on her place on the couch next to the oven, and with a low voice was uncovering wonderful new worlds in front of the sparkling eyes of her grandchildren.

143

> *The story finished, but they still sat noiseless,*
> *staring at their mezmama.*
>
> *The warm, comfortable kitchen was filled*
> *with silence. Only the kettle on the oven was*
> *singing.*

Wow, it's wonderful! Eric thought, and then read it again, slowly.

Bravo, Alexa!

Just like magic, it took him back to their childhood in the backyard of their house. Eric again saw the beautiful gardens, the flowers, and the trees. He heard their happy voices. He remembered the games, and again saw his grandmother, Arakssi. All these scenes made him happy and gave him so much joy!

Eric was also pleased that with his writing, he gave courage to his cousin Alexa to share her memories. They were written so well, and with such pure feelings and love.

Eric called her, and she was very excited and happy that he liked her writing. He encouraged her to send them to his sister Lisa and her father as well.

"I'm sure they will love your short stories. Your father will feel good, and he will definitely be proud of you."

"Thank you, Eric, for your support," Alexa answered. As I told you, they are a bit naive and sentimental, but I do not care. These are my feelings and how I remember our childhood."

"Do not worry, Alexa. It is very good, and I like it as it is. So whenever you can, please keep on writing and keep on sending them to us."

Alexa was moved, and she told him to continue writing as well. Then she told him that her father was reading his book and soon would call him.

On the next day, Eric spoke with his uncle.

"Eric, I have a few recommendations for you," his uncle said right after they exchanged greetings.

"First, the book is not finished yet. Write more about your family—Renee, Nevena, Maya. Write details about the beginning of your emigration—the first night, the first week, the first year. I suppose people remember best the beginning of the emigration, when things are drastically different and difficult. I do not know this. You need to tell us how it was!

"Write about your mother, Nelly. She was the backbone of your family!

"Write more about your father, and write about your sister Lisa and her husband, Arak. Write about your nephew, Joe!

"I suggest you do not write any more about Dave.

"Now, coming back to what you have written.

"When you started the story about your great-grandmother Ovsana, you are talking about her brother and how you do not know his name. I forgot it, but I used to know it. Why did you call him Garabed? This

145

is a very ordinary name, often used in Radio Yerevan jokes."

Eric quickly said, "This is exactly why I chose it, because the name does not make the person, and I wanted to use an ordinary name if I could not use his real name."

"I sent you a family tree a few years ago," his uncle continued. "Read it again. There should be the names of her brothers and when they died.

"He was not an ordinary man. He was a brave man. My memories are telling me that my grandmother's brother joined Antranik, but he fought for Armenia on the east side of Turkey during the Turkish-Russian War. He died much later, in 1919, and not on the Bulgarian-Turkish front in 1913, as you are suggesting.

"Also, write a little bit about your grandfather Agop's mother—my grandmother, Armine. She came to Plovdiv with Harry when they left Istanbul. She helped Agop and practically saved his life.

"He was sick with typhus when he arrived in Bulgaria and managed to find them in Plovdiv. If it were not for his mother, Armine, and his brother Harry, the doctors would have put him in a common barracks with hundreds of other sick people. They were dying like flies.

"She risked her life and stayed with Agop in a separate room kept for officers. She was regularly checking his temperature. He had a fever of 40 degrees Celsius, and she was able to keep his temperature down by wrapping his burning, weak body with cold, wet sheets. She stayed there for thirty days, till the doctors let them go home with no fear for his life or for spreading the infection."

"Did you know this story?" Uncle Ed asked him.

"Yes, I knew it. I will write about it later. I will see how to connect it with the rest of the stories," Eric said.

"Eric, you need to find a good editor to help you with the grammar, one who can give you good advice on how to structure the book. In some places, you need to improve your writing.

"At the end, I can say that the book is good! I like your style of not giving too many details, and I like the short stories. I'm curious to see how you will continue with it," Uncle Ed said.

"Continue writing, and call me when you need me!" He finished talking about the book.

"Okay, uncle. I will call you back after I go over your recommendations and my notes," Eric said. Not long after that, he closed the telephone.

Eric's head was burning.

How is it possible that I forgot about the family tree he gave me a few years ago? I'm writing a book about my grandparents, and I did not check my uncle's family tree. He felt really embarrassed.

Actually, I did not forget it, but I was thinking I knew it by heart. Now my uncle has reminded me that I need to read it again more carefully.

Right away Eric went to the attic, where his office was, and opened the file where he kept his uncle's letters and printed e-mails.

Here were the family trees of the Azadian family and the Kaladian family, prepared by Edwin Azadian.

Eric took in his hands the Kaladian family tree—*my Grandmother Ovsana's line.* His uncle had written:

- Father—Nigohos Hadjiahparian was born in 1855 in Yozgat, Turkey. Died in 1914 in Turkey.
- Mother—Surpohy Hadjiahparian was born in 1860 in Yozgat, Turkey. Died in 1914 in Turkey.

Their kids were:

- Ardashes Hadjiahparian, born in 1890 in Yozgat, Turkey. Died in 1919 in Turkey.
- Ovsana Hadjiahparian, born in 1892 in Yozgat, Turkey. Died in 1941 in Plovdiv, Bulgaria.
- Sarkis Hadjiahparian, born in 1894 in Yozgat, Turkey. Died in 1915 in Turkey.
- Merriam Hadjiahparian, born in 1896 in Yozgat, Turkey. Died in 1915 in Turkey.

My God, most of my family was erased in the short period of time from 1914 to 1915. This was the prewar time with Russia. What could they possibly do so wrong that they were killed?

Nigohos was fifty-nine, his wife Surpohy fifty-four, and their kids Sarkis and Merriam only twenty-one and nineteen years old. Surely they were peaceful citizens of the Ottoman Empire. Why were they killed?

Was it because Turkey wanted to get rid of the Armenians before they entered World War I so they wouldn't lose East Turkey as they did the lands in the European part of the Ottoman Empire in 1913, when they lost the Balkan War against Bulgaria, Greece, Serbia, and Montenegro?

Only Ardashes and Ovsana survived the Armenian genocide. Ardashes died somewhere in Turkey, most probably at the end of the Turkey-Russian War in 1919.

So, my great-granduncle was Ardashes Hadjiahparian. This was the man who helped my great-grandmother Ovsana and her two small children to escape from Turkey and settle in Bulgaria. This was the man who fought together with the legendary Antranik Pasha for the freedom of Armenia.

My uncle thought that Antranik was fighting only in East Turkey, and that is why Ardashes could have joined him there and maybe never went to Bulgaria.

He said that maybe Ovsana and her two children came to Bulgaria later, not in 1912.

My memories from the stories of my grandmother are different. Was I wrong?

I do not think so.

She couldn't travel with two small kids through the Ottoman Empire after the Balkan War started in October 1912.

There were 500,000 Turkish soldiers and 700,000 Bulgarian, Serbian, Greek, and Montenegrin soldiers on the European side, and another 500,000 more Turkish soldiers waiting to get in the war on the Asian side of the Ottoman Empire. The war continued in 1913, and then the First World War started in 1914. The war for Turkey continued till 1922. So how could Ovsana go to Jerusalem and then to Cairo and then to Varna in Bulgaria?

I clearly remember seeing my grandmother's tattoos on her hands and wrists, and I remember her story of visiting Jerusalem and Cairo. I remember her telling me that when she came to Bulgaria, she was six years old and her brother was three years old. I remember her saying that when she was born, her mother was fourteen years old.

It makes sense. My grandmother was born in 1906 and her mother, Ovsana, in 1892 according to the family tree. So in 1912, when they arrived in Bulgaria, Ovsana was twenty years old and my grandmother, Arakssi, was six years old.

Eric opened the computer and started searching for anything on Andranik Pasha or General Andranik.

There was plenty of information in English. He stayed up almost all night reading and searching for more articles about Antranik. Bulgarians and Russians were calling him Antranik instead of Andranik.

All Eric had known about Antranik Pasha was that he was an Armenian hero, who fought for Armenian liberation from the Ottoman Empire, but he discovered much more about him.

Eric felt proud that his great-uncle Ardashes was one of the 270 volunteer warriors who, during the Balkan War and later during the First World War, fought next to Antranik Pasha for the liberation of the West Armenia in East Turkey.

He was kind of surprised that his uncle didn't know that his granduncle Ardashes participated in the Balkan War. He only told Eric that Ardashes fought with Antranik in East Turkey, participated in the war between Russia and Turkey, and died in 1919 in East Turkey.

It is strange how little the Bulgarian history books talked about Antranik Pasha.

Eric decided to check on the Internet using the Bulgarian language. He checked the websites of Bulgarian public libraries for more information.

He ran the search engine in Bulgarian and got more details about Antranik Pasha during the Balkan War from 1912 to 1913 and about the rest of his life.

Eric found out that Antranik Pasha helped supply weapons during the preparation of the Ilinden Uprising in 1903. He bought weapons outside Bulgaria and smuggled them into the country, hiding them in an abandoned field located on the Black Sea coast not far from Varna.

He sent them to Macedonian warriors in Ohrid, as well as Armenians in West Armenia to support the partisan war inside the Ottoman Empire.

In the fall of 1912, Bulgaria, Greece, Serbia, and Montenegro started a war against Turkey. Then the headquarters of the Macedonian-Adrianopolitan militia invited Antranik to join the Bulgarian Army.

Antranik agreed, and with his 270 people, on October 3, 1912, officially joined the Bulgarian Army.

December 2011

On December 9, Eric arrived for a weeklong visit at Chennai, or as some people still calls it, Madras, on the southeast coast of India. It is the capital of the province of Tamil Nadu. He visited an engineering show; he wanted to see and feel how the industry was developing in India. He didn't know what to expect, and for him this was quite a change seeing a new world he had never visited before.

He couldn't find anything interesting in terms of business, but most probably he was not ready for it. He was not sure what he was looking for career-wise. He was not ready to start a business, but he was tempted. He saw young people full of energy and enthusiasm looking for new opportunities. This was basically a trip that gave him a chance to change his thoughts and ideas.

He met different people, made some new friends, and visited Indian museums and temples. He was amazed at the richness of the Indian culture and the variety of colors he saw around him. He wasn't pleased by the noise of the cars on the streets. It seemed like they wouldn't move if they didn't honk all the time. He saw the modern world and old traditions mixed together. He felt the richness and the poverty around him at every street he visited. He was amazed to see poor people very happy and smiling and enjoying life.

From his contacts with the local people, he never heard a word from anybody complaining how little money they had. Everybody was smiling, and they were polite with him. They were happy, and they were honest.

He went to an Indian spa, which was strongly recommended by an Indian exhibitor during his visit to the engineering show.

Everything was well arranged, but there was no locker where he could put his clothes, documents, and money.

"Just leave your baggage with us," the personnel working in the room told him. "Do not worry, sir. Nobody will touch them. Please take off your rings as well from your fingers and put them in your pocket. And you have to take off all your clothes."

They massaged his body from the roots of the hair on his head to the toes of his feet using a special palm oil.

"This is strong oil, sir. When you go home, you will sleep twelve hours. You will feel like a newborn."

Once the massage was over, they gave him soap and a towel, and he entered the next room to take a shower. He was worried about his documents and money.

When he came out, he saw the Indian personnel standing next to the chair with his clothes on it.

He quickly put on his clothes. All his documents were there.

"Sir, please do not forget to put on your golden rings. They must be in your pocket."

Eric put his wedding ring back on, as well as the ring with a black stone that he had received as a present from his wife.

He felt a bit uncomfortable doubting the honesty of these men. But he was still discovering India. This was his first trip there.

He thanked them, left them good tips, and went out. His friend Patel was still in the spa, not rushing to come out.

The next day was his last day before going back to Canada. His friends took him to Marina Beach. It was something to be seen. The English boulevard ran parallel with the beach. Beautiful houses built during the last few centuries were all along it. The beach itself was wide, at least five hundred meters, maybe more. They took a taxi right from the exhibition complex to the beach, and he was wearing his suit and tie. It was hot, maybe 30 degrees Celsius. He took off his tie and his shoes and started walking right at the edge of the sandy beach, touching the water of the Indian Ocean.

An old Indian woman came and begged for money. He gave her some, and she wished him health and long life.

A tall white horse was galloping toward them, and a young Indian man jumped off a few meters away from them.

His Indian friend Patel was laughing. "It looks you are attracting the attention of the locals."

"What does he want?" Eric asked.

"He wants to take you for a ride so he can make some money for him and his horse," Patel said.

Then he said something to the rider and turned back to Eric smiling. "He said that you Americans ride horses only in the movies, and he is asking if you would be afraid to mount this horse."

"Wow! Is he challenging me?" Eric asked.

"Yes, can you ride?" Patel asked.

"Yes, I've ridden a few times, but not on a horse like this," Eric said, looking with admiration at the tall legs and the thin muscled body of the horse. The horse was keeping its head up and watching him as well.

"Good horse. Good horse!" The Indian was tapping the horse's back with one hand while holding red reins attached to his head. A tall old saddle was mounted on his back.

"Try it. He will take you behind him," Patel said.

"Okay. How much do you want for me riding it alone?" Eric asked directly to the horseman.

"No, sir, not alone," he said, still smiling.

"I will be alone, or I will not ride it," Eric said.

"Okay, sir, but go not far and not fast. I want one hundred rupees, sir."

"I have only eighty," Eric said.

"Okay, sir; you gave twenty to my mother." He was still smiling, and he lowered one side of the reins attached to the side of the saddle where the stirrup was.

Eric put his leg on the stirrup, and holding the reins attached to the horse's head, he mounted in one motion, sitting tall in the saddle.

"What is his name?"

"Rocky," the Indian answered. "Please, sir. Go slowly and only two hundred meters and come back. I will be running right behind you," he said without smiling anymore and with some worry in his eyes.

Eric first tapped the neck of the horse a few times, calling him by his name and saying the same things repeatedly. "Good horse. Rocky, you are a good horse. We will ride together."

He was holding the reins tight, not letting him run, but just walk in the beginning. Then he stopped him and made him turn a full 360 degrees in one place, and then he let the reins fall loosely and whispered in the horse's ear, "Okay. Rocky, gallop! Run, run!" and he touched him with the rear edge of his shoes on his belly on both sides.

The horse started galloping, leaving far behind the young man, now shouting in panic. The Indian was worried about him. Only now did he notice that the stirrup on Rocky's left side was too long and he couldn't step on it when the horse slowed down in trotting. Eric pulled the reins strongly, and the horse stopped. But Rocky was still fighting with the reins and started turning to the direction of the wide beach. He wanted to run. Finally the young man came and tried to catch the reins of the horse. Eric let the reins loose maybe just a fraction of a second too quickly before the Indian man could have a full grip on them. The horse jumped forward, pushing the Indian man on one side on the ground and galloping up the slope of the beach.

Eric quickly bent forward, unable to step on his feet in both stirrups at the same time, but he squeezed the sides of the horse between his legs and kept himself straight. When the horse reached the end of the slope of the beach, Eric pulled strongly on the reins, and the horse stopped immediately. He was not happy, but he obeyed. The horse stood up on his rear legs while pawing the air with his front legs.

"Calm down, Rocky! Calm down!" Eric was whispering now in his ears and tapping on his neck.

The Indian man came up, and this time he got the reins in his hand while Eric jumped down. He was smiling again.

Patel also came up and gave him back his camera. "Well, it looks like you knew how to ride a horse. You made a small show here," he said, motioning around, where a few Indian families were still watching them.

Eric looked at them and noticed a tall man standing out a few steps from the locals. His white clothes were long and loose. His long beard was waving with the wind. Their eyes met for a moment, and then the man picked up his right hand in a greeting. Eric did the same.

"Who is that tall man?" Eric turned to Patel to ask.

"I see no tall man," Patel said.

Eric turned, but he saw only the local Indian people.

"Strange. He was right there just a few seconds ago. It doesn't matter," Eric said. "Did you at least take pictures of me galloping?" he asked.

"Honestly, I was so shocked, I forgot about the camera. I took a few in the beginning." Patel was excusing himself.

"That's okay. As you can see, us Americans, we know how to ride," Eric said calmly, but his legs were still shaking from the adrenalin.

Later the same day, they visited other tourist sites not far from the same beach.

Eric was surprised to find out that there was the tomb of St. Thomas. He visited the gorgeous church of St. Thomas and his tomb. There were many tourists, as well as local Indian Christians.

Eric was standing in the church, and in front of him was a glass floor. Below it was the tomb of St. Thomas. He didn't know that St. Thomas went to the east to preach Christianity, and here on the southeast coast of India, he was martyred.

Eric felt strange standing in this church. This church had a great importance for Christianity. He came here without knowing that the tomb of St. Thomas was there.

What chance! Eric thought, and he silently prayed. To his surprise, he also saw Patel praying on his knees. On his way out, he told himself how lucky he was to come here. He felt he was blessed.

A few hours later, he was pleasantly surprised to find out that one of the tourist places was the Armenian church, located on the Armenian street not too far from Marina Beach. This was a church built by Armenian merchants who came from Iran about three hundred years ago. They settled in Madras with their families, and the community prospered for centuries. They helped the local Indian people. They built streets, houses, and a bridge that is still functional today. The church was freshly renovated with funds from Armenia and was very attractive in architectural style.

The church was run by local Indian people, who greeted him with respect when they found out that Eric was an Armenian from Canada. Eric learned that the local Armenians had mostly moved to California in America and some to Calcutta in India. He felt kind of sad standing there with no Armenians around. The Indian guide took him to the tomb of the Armenian who established the first printing company in India.

Eric silently prayed for the descendants of the Armenians who built this church and the street with the bridge and for the descendants of the first Armenian entrepreneurs in India to be well and happy wherever they had found their new homes and country. He prayed as well for his family to be well and happy and for him to determine what he was looking for.

On December 16, Eric returned home. His family was waiting for him. Renee was happy that he came home healthy and in a good mood. Eric felt comfortable with the idea that he would not start a business. He felt very good being at home with his family, among the people he loved the most.

The whole family gathered together for Christmas.

This is what I'm looking for—the happiness of all of them, Eric thought while looking around himself at the smiling faces.

September 1913

Ovsana looked at her two children. Arakssi was now seven years old and Hagop four. Almost a year had passed since they came to Bulgaria and five months since they moved to Plovdiv.

She was well accepted in the Armenian community there. An old Armenian woman, Diguin (Mm) Hripssimes, took them into her house. She was a widow.

Hripssimes's children had grown up and gotten married in France, where they were graduate students ten years earlier. She missed them, and she missed her grandchildren. She wanted to sell the house and live with her children in Paris, but the Balkan War had started and she had to stay in Bulgaria. When the priest spoke with her about Ovsana and her small kids, she was glad to offer them a room in her house.

Ovsana was happy to stay with Diguin Hripssimes; it felt like being at home. The house was in the old city, located on a small hill overlooking the new Plovdiv.

The Armenian church and school were just a few blocks away from home. Every morning she took her children to the school, and after work she picked them up. She started working at the military hospital as a sanitarian. The barracks of the hospital were about four kilometers west from the old city of Plovdiv, on the south side of the Maricza River. It was wartime, and they needed every person who had some experience.

In the beginning, she was afraid that they would not accept her since she didn't know Bulgarian. She remembered her first visit to the hospital.

The doctor in charge told her in good Turkish, "You can speak Turkish in the beginning, but do not forget to say that you are Armenian." Then he smiled and explained that Bulgaria got its independence from Turkey about five years earlier.

He continued, "Just four months ago, we were at war with them for liberation of the remaining Bulgarian territories.

"Almost everybody over forty years old speaks Turkish, but they will pretend they do not understand it. The younger generation may not know how to speak it, but they will understand you. Just say that you are an Armenian emigrant from Turkey, and they will accept you and will communicate with you in Turkish."

He invited her to sit in the chair in front of his desk and continued. "The priest told me that you have experience as a sanitarian and have worked in a hospital in Jerusalem."

"Yes, but I worked at the hospital for only two months. Then I had to follow my brother to Bulgaria. He came here as a volunteer to fight for liberation of Armenia. He joined the Bulgarian Army." Ovsana lost her voice and looked to one side, trying to hide her emotions. She didn't take the seat and was standing in front of the doctor.

"Yes, I know. The priest told me." He stood up, and with a softer voice, said, "Your experience is good enough for me.

You can start tomorrow morning at 8:00 a.m."

"That is okay with me, but can I leave at 5:00 p.m.? I have to pick up my kids from school and do my work at home."

"That is fine. I'll see you tomorrow morning." He shook her hand.

"Start learning Bulgarian." He gave her a friendly smile and wished her a good day.

She came back from her memories. She was at home and was looking at her kids. She was thinking about their future. How could she manage with everything? How could they continue living in Bulgaria?

Everything seemed to be well; only the emigration officer was giving her a hard time. He wanted to send them back to Turkey.

He said that they did not have proper documents and she had entered Bulgaria as a visitor and could not stay.

She told him that it was wartime. They would be risking their lives if they went back, and she wanted to have refugee status.

Then she told him about her brother, who came to Bulgaria to fight for

Bulgaria. She told him that her brother was pronounced missing or dead, together with many other Armenians who joined the Bulgarian Army, and she told him about the officer who promised the remaining relatives that they would receive Bulgarian citizenship.

The emigration officer told her that there was no proof that she was the sister and that was why he could not do anything.

On the next day, he came to her house. She was surprised and didn't know what to expect.

"Mr. Prodanov, what are you doing here?" Ovsana asked with a note of disbelief in her voice.

"I have good news for you and maybe I can help you, but I need to give money to the right people to get you the proper documents." He smiled at her, but looking hungrily with his eyes at her.

She stepped back, and he entered the house.

"You Armenians, you have golden coins. Give me two golden coins, and I will be able to convince the office manager and you will have no problems anymore."

Ovsana was not expecting this.

"I … I do not have so much money. I'll have to work two years to be able to earn this kind of money," Ovsana said in horror.

"I'm sorry, but this cannot wait so long. I will come next week at the same time, and if you cannot find two golden Turkish coins, I cannot help you." He turned and started to leave, but then he remembered something. He stopped and came back to her—too close for her to feel comfortable—and added, "By the way, do not say anything to anybody, because then nobody will be able to help you" He looked at her eyes with icy coldness and touched her face with the back of his hand. "Remember, golden Turkish coins only!"

Then he looked at the table and said, "You have a beautiful tablecloth. Is it handmade? Is that Armenian?"

"Yes, my mother made it for me. It is handmade," she answered, pulling away from him.

"May I?" he said, and he took it with him on his way out.

Ovsana was terrified. She shivered. His touch was even colder than his words and his eyes. She was scared, and she was upset. He was trying to get money from her. How could she find two golden coins?

She had to speak with somebody. She needed advice or at least some kind of hope. What if they really were going to extradite her back to Turkey?

"No," she said to herself "I'm not taking my children back there. I will find these two golden coins even if I have to work for only food and shelter till I pay them back."

Ovsana was afraid to speak to anyone, but keeping her mouth shut was not going to help her either.

She told Diguin Hripssimes what had happened and asked her for advice.

After staying up late almost the whole night, they decided that the best thing was to speak again with the Armenian priest. He knew many influential people in both the Armenian and Bulgarian communities.

The next day the priest carefully wrote down the name of the emigration officer and told her that this was not the first time he was receiving complaints from widows or single families that had no man to protect them.

"It is time to put a stop to this," he said to himself.

To Ovsana he said, "Do not worry, my child. I'm glad you came to see me. Come back in three days; I will find you the money, and you will give it to him."

Mr. Prodanov returned after the week had passed. It was already turning dark outside, and when she opened the door, she couldn't see him well at the beginning. There was another man with him, but she couldn't see his face.

"Wait for me outside," he said to his companion and entered the room.

"Good evening, my dear. How are you?" He smiled at her with his snake's eyes.

He carefully looked around the room and then closed the door and locked it from inside. "Where are your kids?" he asked.

"They are with my neighbor."

"Good. Did you find the money?"

"Yes, but I had to borrow it. I will have to work a few years to pay them back."

"I do not care. This is your problem. I'm not forcing you. As you can see, I'm just trying to help you," he said, trying to convince her how good a person he was.

"If I give you this money, can you guarantee me that I will receive refugee status and be accepted to become a Bulgarian citizen?" Ovsana asked suddenly, without any signs of fear.

He looked at her a little bit surprised.

"Do you have the coins with you, or not?" he almost shouted at her.

"Yes, I do, but you did not answer my question."

"Do not play games with me! Show them to me!" Now he was not pretending anymore to be a good man; he was angrily glaring at her.

"Mr. Prodanov, what is making you so angry? If you cannot give me any guarantee, why do I have to give you these golden coins? I'd rather give them to your boss if he is the one giving the approval. Doesn't this make any sense to you?"

Ovsana seemed like a different person to him, and he looked at her as if seeing her for the first time.

Then the anger came over him again—stronger than his suspicions—and he shouted at her.

"You little Armenian woman, don't you understand that everything depends on me? I'm the one who can give you the approval or send you back."

"Please don't. I will give you the money," she whispered with a shaking voice, and she gave him the two golden coins.

He approached her angrily and grabbed her blouse.

"Yes, you will give me the money, and not only that." Now his intentions were more than obvious. He tore her blouse and forced her down to the bed.

"No, what are you doing? Stop! Leave me alone!" Ovsana cried loudly, fighting him back and clawing his face.

"Help, help!" she cried out.

"You!" he shouted and slapped her face in anger.

At this moment, the door flew open, broken from the frame, and two men ran into the room.

Before Prodanov understood what was happening, four strong hands pulled him up from the bed and threw him onto a chair, quickly tying his hands behind the back of the chair.

Ovsana saw two men, one dressed in a Bulgarian Army officer uniform; the other man immediately drew her attention because he was dressed in the black clothes of an Armenian warrior. His wide shoulders were covered with gray pelerine, and his hood covered his head; only his slightly curved nose and curly black beard were visible. While they moved quickly to apprehend Prodanov, his pelerine opened a few times and she saw that he carried a long dagger and a pistol in his thin red waistcloth. His legs were in tall black leather boots.

The Bulgarian officer was shouting something in Bulgarian. He was probably in his early thirties, and his well-shaved face had turned red in obvious anger. He was slim and tall, about a full head taller than the Armenian. But the Armenian warrior was the one who was radiating indisputable power, and his swift movements around the room away and close to Prodanov were full of anger.

Prodanov's wide eyes watched the Armenian with fear; he realized who was more dangerous.

Suddenly the Bulgarian officer started talking in decent Turkish.

"Yes, look at him well, because if I give you to him, he will cut you in small pieces. You are a shame to the Bulgarian nation.

"How could you do that? While all the brave Bulgarian men were fighting for the liberation of our territories and nation, you were blackmailing, abusing, and robbing women and single mothers with no protection. Do you know who these people are?" He gestured at Ovsana and then at the Armenian man while looking at Prodanov.

"*Idiot takuv!* You are such an idiot! *Kak moja da go napravish?* How could you do that?" He was mixing Bulgarian and Turkish words.

He stopped for a moment, taking a deep breath, and continued, not really expecting any answer:

"Their brothers, husbands, and fathers came here as volunteers to fight for our and their liberation. They are heroes. They are brave and fearless warriors, and it is my privilege to fight next to them. Have you heard of General Antranik?"

Prodanov's face turned yellow in panic.

"I see you know about him. His battalion was the tip of our sword in every attack against the Turkish positions. Every battle they participated in, we won.

"They were the first to enter one of the strongest fortresses in Europe—Edirne. They opened the door for us so we could enter and fight inside the fortress. This was an impossibly great victory for the Bulgarian Army. Yaver Pasha, with ten thousand soldiers from the Turkish regular army, surrendered."

He stopped shouting and continued in a low voice, "Her brother was one of these Armenian warriors who made history for our nation. And you, piece of dirt, were trying to rape her."

A sound of deep pain came from the chest of the Armenian. He halfway drew the dagger and came close to Prodanov.

Prodanov looked in horror at the blood dripping from one of the Armenian's fingers; trying to hold himself back, he had cut himself without realizing it. The effort was expressive. He was not talking, just breathing heavily.

The Bulgarian officer broke the silence.

"Prodanov, I can help you save your miserable life and redeem yourself, but you have to sign up as a volunteer in the Bulgarian Army, and you have to return the money you stole from all the emigrants."

Prodanov turned his face with some hope and said, "Is that for real?"

"Yes, here is the contract; you have to sign it now." He took some papers from his bag.

"I'm authorized to recruit volunteers in the army under my command. If you survive the war, you will come back with a clean record."

"Can you guarantee me that he is not going to kill me after I give the money back?" Prodanov asked, looking at the Armenian warrior.

The Bulgarian officer interrupted. "Do not play games with me. Do you want to volunteer or not? I do not have time to waste with you, and believe me, I'm not having fun in your company."

He turned to the Armenian warrior and said, "Brother, he is yours,"

"Wait, wait! Give me this paper. I will sign it right away."

The Bulgarian officer turned toward the open door and shouted an order in Bulgarian. A sergeant came in and stood still.

"Sergeant Petrov, take this man with you. He is now a volunteer in our army. Watch him closely, and if he tries to escape, shoot him. I will join you in an hour at our base. You know what to do with him."

"Yes, sir, and I have here one more volunteer. This is the guy who came with Prodanov. I will take them both to the base and wait for your next orders."

Finally there were just Ovsana and the two men who saved her in the room.

"Ovsana," the Bulgarian officer said as he turned to her, "I'm sorry I did not present myself, but in these circumstances, you will understand I am taking my first opportunity to do that.

"I'm Lieutenant Methody Terziev from the Macedonian-Adrianopolitan Volunteer Corps of the Bulgarian Army. I served together with your brother, Ardashes. It is a pleasure and an honor to meet you, madam."

Then he turned to the Armenian to introduce him, but he realized he didn't know what to say. "Here is a good friend of mine, more a brother to me. Let him present himself to you."

Ovsana looked at the Armenian, but he didn't pick up his head and didn't open his hood. Suddenly he turned and started walking out.

"Ardashes, *tun es?* Is that you?" Ovsana cried in Armenian.

He stopped for a moment without turning, and then he quickly walked out.

"I'm sorry," Lieutenant Terziev told her, and then he placed the two golden coins on the table and said, "These are your money, Ovsana. Your brother wanted you to have them."

"Who is that man? Why is he not talking? Why is he not showing his face to me?"

"I … I don't know why, madam, but I'm sure there is a reason."

"If he is not my brother, then where is my brother? Why is he not contacting me?"

Ovsana took Terziev's arm and said, "Thank you for your help. I can imagine what would have happened if you had not come."

Then she begged him, "Please tell me more about my brother. Where is he?"

"Officially he is missing or dead, together with the rest of the Antranik warriors."

Lieutenant Terziev suddenly looked down to the ground, not feeling comfortable, but he continued, "When the peace treaty was signed with Turkey, one of the conditions was that Bulgaria had to give them all the Armenian soldiers who fought against Turkey. They were afraid of Antranik Pasha, as they called him.

"Bulgaria at that time was invaded by his allies and had to fight against

Greece, Serbia, Montenegro, and Romania all at the same time. Our ex allies had turned against us because we wanted the biggest share of the territories we took from Turkey. They wanted more land for themselves, even though the biggest victories were won by the Bulgarian Army. Bulgaria had to sign the peace treaty with Turkey to be able to save at least some of the territories that were liberated after the war against Turkey.

"We couldn't, however, betray our friends, the Armenian warriors who helped us in this war. We let them go. Officially we pronounced them dead or missing. Also, the Armenians wanted to continue their fight for liberation of West Armenia. So they left. They disappeared in the nearby mountains between Odrin and the Black Sea. The last time I spoke with Arda, he told me that they would go back to East Turkey to carry on a partisan war till Russia gets involved in the war. This was their last hope for Armenia."

"Is he hiding here in Bulgaria?" Ovsana asked with hope in her voice.

"I cannot say anything more, madam. You understand. But maybe what I told you will give some answers to your previous questions."

He looked her straight in the eyes. "Officially, if we catch him, we must give him to the Turks. You'd be better to not know where he is, as I do not know.

"I'm happy I was able to help you with your problem with the emigration officer, and please accept my apologies on behalf of all Bulgarian soldiers. I will make sure your request for Bulgarian citizenship will be granted soon." Then he saluted her and promised to come and see her when he was again in Plovdiv. Then he left.

Ovsana was burning in the heat of her emotions. She wanted to run after the officer and ask him again where her brother was. She felt that the man in the gray pelerine with the hood was actually Ardashes.

Was he still outside waiting for his friend? Ovsana ran out of the room, but instead of going out from the main entrance of the house, she turned the other way in the corridor and entered the kitchen. There were two windows with metal bars. Both were left open. One looked to the backyard and one to the street. The back door of the house led to the backyard. To access the backyard from the street, one had to first enter through the big metal door on the wall that separated the street from the back.

The room was dark when she entered it, and she looked out the window. There she saw the silhouettes of two men. She heard their low voices.

The taller man was speaking. She concentrated to be able to understand what he was saying.

"I really do not understand why you are so hard to her and yourself. You are leaving tomorrow, and only God knows if you will ever be able to come back and see them …"

"Shh, do not say anything more. Do not make it more difficult. I'm dead for them, and it's better I stay like this. I know I will never come back …" He stopped for a moment and then said, "Thank you for your help, brother. Please protect them if you can …"

"I will, brother. If not me, I mean if I'm not alive, somebody else will. We will never forget what Antranik Pasha and his warriors did for us. When Bulgaria couldn't officially buy the weapons for us, Antranik and his warriors helped us buy the weapons, and then you joined our fight for liberation of the Trace Macedonians. We will never be able to pay you back."

"Yes, you have …"

"No, we haven't …" He hugged his friend good-bye and said, "Go now, and do not be late. The fishing boats are waiting for you not far from the same place you were bringing us the weapons. My people will take you to open sea early in the morning before the sun rises, and then hopefully your Russians will be there as they promised you to take you to the east coast of the Black Sea. From there, you are on your own. God be with you, my brother!"

The two men separated and disappeared in the dark street.

May 15, 2013

Eric came from a meeting with his accountant for the year end of his holding company.

When Renee saw him entering the house, she right away said to him, "I can see he was pushing you again to invest our money in a business. I told you to get somebody else. There are so many other good accountants. Since you do not have an active company, it is becoming easier and easier for him. Maybe that's why he insists you buy a Subway restaurant or a block of apartments or start any business—so he can charge you more money. They all think only about themselves, and not really about you, unlike what he probably told you. Do not be naive. Nobody thinks about your good. They only see your money. He doesn't care if we have to take a new loan out and work again as hard as we used to—or even if we lose money."

Eric was listening and not saying anything, and Renee was getting even more upset.

"No, he didn't talk about this," Eric lied. "He just prepared all the year-end papers and explained the numbers to me. The company is issuing regular dividends, which will help us till next year. I will continue paying us small salaries." Eric was explaining in detail what was important for them.

Renee listened carefully, but her face still showed that she was worried how they would manage till they got to sixty-five years old, when they would get pensions from the Revenue Agency of Ontario and from Canada's old-age security program.

"Do not worry!" Eric said with a calm voice, trying to influence her.

"How can I not worry when I see how easily he can manipulate you? You have a tendency to believe what people tell you. You are not worldly. I always told you, you are too good of a person to be able to run a business."

"Relax, I'm not planning to open a business. I'm just planning to do nothing for now, and then just roll on my back and pretend I'm dead ..." Now Eric was getting upset.

"What make you think that I'm naïve?" Eric shouted.

"Because you spend your money too freely, and sometimes you just give it away," Renee said.

"Do you remember when you were working at Seda how many times you personally gave money to employees? You helped people you had to let go, or others because they left the country and went back home to their countries. You helped others because their wives left them or because their parents passed away, or because his wife was sick and he was laid off and didn't have money for his kids, or because somebody was robbed on the way home and you gave him the money back, or because I do not know what else ..." Renee was raising her voice.

"So what? I gave them a little money so they could feel good. So they could feel that somebody else cared about them. Big deal. Does that make me naïve, or just a man with a heart?" Eric looked at his wife closely. "This didn't bother you before. What is happening to you?"

"How about all the money and the time you gave to the church? Is that also what you call a little money?" Renee was not giving up. Now she was shouting also.

"Yes, I changed because I'm afraid that soon we will not have money and then we will both have to go to work again. You are fifty-eight years old, and you are tired and you cannot sleep well. You are forgetting quickly how difficult it was for you the last few years. How desperately you wanted to stop working. Yes, I'm afraid that you will promise something, and then you will have to do it as you always do. But you cannot now. You will kill yourself. Your nerves and your health are not the same anymore. You are taking handfuls of pills at a time. I ... I cannot live if you die ..." Now Renee started crying.

Eric came closer and gently hugged her. "Relax. You are jumping to conclusions too fast. I'm not naïve. I know what I'm doing, and also, as I always did, I will not do something without you knowing about and agreeing to it. Just trust me," Eric said and looked her in the eyes.

"I know we are both tired and our nerves are not very good, so I'm not crazy about jumping into a business. I do not think I will be able to manage it, but yes, I'm tempted, and yes, I would do something if you would just tell me, 'Go ahead. I believe in you. You can do it,'" Eric said calmly.

"*I'm* afraid also. It's not only you. I'm worried about you as well, and I can see how thin your nerves are, how easily you can get upset and sick." He hugged her gently and kissed her on the top of her head.

"Do not worry. I will not let anybody else influence me to start a business or invest in something risky— nothing that will enslave us back to working such long hours." Eric stopped for a moment while looking at Renee.

"Do not worry. I'm working as a consultant on engineering projects at least three days per week. I'm also managing our investments on the stock market. I believe we will be good till we get retired, and then we have our registered retirement saving plans (RRSP). So we are doing okay, my dear."

"So, why don't you tell him directly not to push you anymore?" Renee asked him, already relaxed.

"First, out of respect for the man, and second, because this is his job. It is up to us to decide what's good for us. He cannot be a good accountant if he thinks only about himself. He thinks about his customers as well. He is certainly trying to help them grow their companies; in this way, he can grow as well. It is against his philosophy to help a company slowly become smaller and then in ten years just stop working. If everybody did this, in ten years he would be out of business ..." They both started laughing.

July 2013

Eric, Renee, and Nina had been on their vacation almost four weeks.

Nina was crying when she stepped out of the plane and stood on Bulgarian land. She was happy to be back there, but sad that this time she was without her husband. Nikola passed away in September 2012 after a long fight with cancer. He was eighty years old.

What can you do? This is life, and time goes on, with or without you …

Eric and Renee convinced Nina to go to Bulgaria with them. They were hoping she could change her mood and start smiling again.

The first week, they spent visiting relatives and Nina's old friends. They went to Plovdiv and Sofia. Then they went to Karlovo so Nina could see her husband's relatives, and then to Tvurdiza, where they met with her sister and her brother.

Finally Nina came back to Karlovo and stayed with relatives and friends. She had lived here with her husband for forty-two years. She knew many people and she had many family friends, as it is in small cities. Slowly she started smiling again. She was happy to be among old friends and relatives.

The second week, Eric and Renee were able to go to their apartment in Sunny Beach. The first few days they were alone, but then Eric's sister Lisa and her husband, Arak, came to see them. It became a tradition for Eric and Renee to come on vacation before July 5, so they could be together for a few days during Lisa's birthday.

This time the restaurant was right on the beach, and they enjoyed the beautiful view of the sea. The old city of Nessebar was on the right side, and the Balkan mountain dove into the Black Sea from the left side, where the city of Saint Vlas had grown up the hills.

It was strange. There were no Bulgarians in the restaurant except the working personnel.

Most of the tourists they met earlier on the beach were foreigners from the European Union or Russia. Eric shared his observation with Lisa and Arak.

"What's going on?" Eric asked.

"Well, people are getting poor, and Sunny Beach became too expensive for them. Don't you watch the demonstrations and protests every evening of thousands of people in the main streets of Sofia? It's all over the news," Lisa said.

"Yes, of course, but I thought it was because the Socialist Party came back into power and formed a coalition with two opposing parties, one representing the Turkish minority in Bulgaria and the other one representing the nationalists," Eric said.

"Yes, that is an absurd coalition, which proves once more that these politicians are too hungry for power and money and do not actually care about their political programs and the people they represent," Arak added.

Arak explained, "Gerb was the only political party that worked for the interests of Bulgaria. The majority government was building highways financed 80 percent by the EU. The problem is that the economy in general in the EU is weak and unemployment in Bulgaria is more than 20 percent."

"If it was doing such a good job, why couldn't Gerb win the elections?" Renee asked.

"I'm not saying that Gerb did not make mistakes. They did. They did not pay enough attention to the socially weak in Bulgaria, and this cost them the elections," Lisa said.

"No, no, Gerb would have won if it was not for the lies and manipulations of the communists." Arak was getting emotional now.

"People in Bulgaria have lost confidence in the political parties because of constant negative remarks and accusations from Bulgarian Socialist Party (BSP) against Gerb without any proof. People are not stupid, and they see and feel everything on their back." Arak paused, trying to find new arguments.

"I was talking with one of the lifeguards earlier today on the beach, and he said something interesting about life in Bulgaria," Eric said.

"A tourist from the EU had told him, 'When poverty starts blowing in under the door, love flies out of the window.'"

Eric looked at Lisa, Arak, and Renee, and said, "Let's drink for the love never to leave our hearts!" He was trying to change the topic.

"And the hearts of all Bulgarians," Lisa added.

They all took a sip from their cups and looked away to the sea. It was getting dark, and stars were starting to become visible in the sky.

"Bulgaria is such a beautiful country, but it looks like she is not able to keep her smart kids," Lisa whispered. Her son, Joe, had been in Calgary, Canada, for more than ten years already.

"Almost every other family has at least one kid in Western Europe or in America. If it were not for them, many old people here would not be able to pay their electricity bills and would stay cold during the winter. But we feel alone ..." Lisa sipped again from her cup filled with Bulgarian rakija.

"Well, Joe has recently started coming back to Bulgaria every year," Renee said.

"I can't complain," Lisa admitted. "But I'm afraid for him when he is there driving his car during the long, cold Canadian winter ..."

"Yes, it's not easy for them. Maya is also alone in Victoria, and we are also afraid for her," Renee said.

"Do not worry about them!" Arak offered. "They will be much better off there than here in Bulgaria. You did well emigrating to Canada twenty-two years ago. I'm sure it was very difficult the first five or ten years, but you are now better off than many are in Bulgaria. Things did not improve much here. We are still seeing the same Communist Party, but now they call themselves socialists. They are masters in political games and intrigues to the point that people in Bulgaria do not know anymore what is a lie and what is true. Corruption rules on all levels of the government, and even though the police arrested all kinds of criminals and crooks, not too many have been brought to justice," Arak said while looking at the sea and the darkening sky.

"This time is different." Arak turned his eyes back to Eric and Renee. "There is hope. Tens of thousands of young, intelligent people are on the streets of Sofia every night, asking for the parliament and government to resign and for new elections. A live river of young people are marching and shouting in front of the parliament in one voice:

"'*Ostavka! Resignation!*'

"This parliament has no future and will come down sooner or later. I do not know when Bulgarians will finally wake up and actively go to vote and clearly demand what they want." Arak was looking upset.

"Let's be optimistic!" Eric said. "Already, the fact that Bulgaria is in the EU is helping the future. Almost a million Bulgarians are working, studying, and living in Europe. This is a major reason for improvement. For me, this is as normal as moving people from small cities and villages to Sofia. Almost one third of the population is living in Sofia, and this is absolutely normal. The investments are there. The big business is in Sofia. The well-paid jobs are in Sofia. It's mostly the old parents and those who are working the land or in tourism at the seacoast and the mountain resorts that remain in the small cities.

"Believe me, in five years, half of the population will be in Sofia. The other half will be divided between the EU and the rest of the country." Eric stopped to see if Arak and Lisa would agree with him. When he saw no negative reaction, he asked, "Who won the elections in Sofia, Plovdiv, Burgas, and Varna?"

"Gerb did," Arak answered.

"Anyway," Arak added, "I'm getting hungry. Let's order!"

Soon they forgot about all the problems, and as all Bulgarians sitting at tables, they started enjoying their food and drinks.

Eric got into his thinking mood again while listening to his relatives order food, and beer with it.

Is that only a Bulgarian syndrome?

So far Bulgarians were famous for their patience. If they had enough food and drinks on the table and they were living under their own roofs, they didn't want to get involved in politics. Somebody else was going to do the political work for them, and they would just complain and be upset with the politicians. How convenient and how naive!

However, a new generation of young people was getting stronger, and they had tasted new fruits—the fruits of freedom, democracy, the free market, and the power and satisfaction of being involved in their own destiny. These people were not going to let any government rule them without really wanting to know in advance what their reaction would be. And this was promising. Soon they would be ready to get involved in the political life of this country. and hopefully they would remain honest and strong against the temptations of corruption.

The Western world did it—why not us? Now we are slowly becoming part of it, aren't we?

"Are you ready to order?" Renee asked him, pulling him from his thoughts.

"I do not know. I'm not very hungry. Let me wait a bit longer while I finish my beer," Eric said.

For a while there was silence at their table, and only the loud music to disturb the pleasant atmosphere in this pretty restaurant. Eric tried to listen to the next tables' conversations. They were attempting to speak louder than the music. Most of them were speaking in Russian, Czech, or Romanian, some in German and in English.

Eric started a new subject. "Yesterday we went to Nessebar to pay our apartment taxes. Half of the people in the municipality waiting to pay their taxes were speaking Russian.

"When we went to the next office to pay for the water tax of our apartment, we were alone with the city clerk. I asked him if he knew how many apartments were sold to foreigners. I was surprised to find out that at least sixty thousand apartments on the Black Sea coast were sold to Russians," Eric said.

"Do you know why so many Russians are buying apartments here?" Eric asked Arak and Lisa.

"I don't know," Arak quickly answered, which sounded more like "I don't want to talk about this right now."

"I will tell you why." Lisa accepted the question, putting down her glass with beer.

"There are a few reasons actually. First, the Black Sea coast of Bulgaria is really beautiful.

"Also, Russians and Bulgarians are reading and writing the same alphabet. Also, it is possible they bought them as investments, expecting prices to jump in the future."

"It is more than that." Arak finally got involved.

"Bulgaria is part of the EU, and many Russians want to get Bulgarian citizenship. Also, they are hungry for democracy. Bulgaria is ahead of Russia and certainly moving faster toward EU democratic values," Arak said.

"There are also thousands of apartments bought by UK citizens. These are mostly people close to their retirement or already retired. They are looking for somewhere with a lot of sunshine, not expensive, politically stable, safe and with friendly people, and not far from home," Lisa added.

"Hopefully Bulgaria will again become a politically stable country. Today it doesn't look like it's very stable, with these weeks of protests of tens of thousands of upset people on the streets," Eric said.

Nobody else said anything, and soon they forgot again about all the problems.

The mood here in the restaurant was good, and everybody around them was enjoying themselves. It was not difficult for them to join in the mood. They ordered more beers and started talking about their plans for the next day. They wanted to drive together south to Sozopol, another ancient city, located about thirty-five kilometers south from Burgas on the Black Sea.

On July 12, Eric and Renee were alone in their apartment.

Renee had decided to stay home one day so she could clean, wash all the clothes and sheets, and put the apartment in order. After she finished with the cleaning, she started cooking.

Eric was happy to stay at home one day and rest from the strong sun on the beach.

He took advantage of this and started writing notes for his book. It had been awhile since he touched his laptop, and now he was eager to again start writing down his observations and thoughts collected during their last four weeks in Bulgaria.

George and Katia, relatives of Renee from Karlovo, visited them for two days. Renee's mother, Nina, had stayed in their apartment for almost a week. It was a pleasure to return the hospitality. Eric was also very interested to speak openly with strong supporters of the BSP and try to understand them.

They didn't like Gerb and its leader, Mr. Borisov, or as they called him, using just his first name, Boyco. They blindly believed the accusation made by BSP that he was a crook. They couldn't accept the fact that the protests in Sofia were coming from intelligent young people who were clearly against BSP and wanted its resignation.

"These are people who are not working; somebody is paying them to protest on the streets," George and Katia argued.

Eric came to realize that people in the small cities supported the socialists and longed for the old days, when everybody was equal in their wealth, or maybe better said, in their poverty. At least it looked like that. Now the society was divided into many extremely poor, some extremely rich, and some in the middle, but these people were living in the big cities, mostly in Sofia.

"Bulgaria is not just Sofia and the big cities," George said. "What about us in the small cities? What are we supposed to do? Factories are either closed or reduced to a few hundred people. Salaries are low, not like in the big cities. Our children are leaving for the big cities or the EU. What will happen with our parents and with us when we retire?" George asked with pain in his voice.

"When Gerb was in power, it was busy building highways and totally forgot about us. How can our parents live with their small pensions? How are we going to live? I have to retire next year, and I'm concerned," George said loudly.

"What's happening in Bulgaria is quite complex." Eric tried to explain what he was seeing.

"Young people are not afraid, and they are leaving the old ways of life. They are heading to the big world, where they expect more. They are learning new languages. They are studying in universities because this will give them better chances. Life is a competition, and the better you are prepared and the harder you work, the better are your chances to live better, to have more, and to get ready for your retirement." Eric was speaking slowly and carefully watching the reactions of George and Katia.

"For some of us, the big world is the bigger city not far from home; for others it is Sofia, and for the most ambitious, it is the EU and America. Do not be afraid of this. People are leaving Bulgaria because they do not have hope here. They will do much better than you did, and they will come back home often to see you, to help you, and maybe to take you with them or to stay with you …"

"I do not understand why the government is not building factories and investing in the small cities. Then our kids would stay home, and we all would have work," George said, interrupting Eric.

"Okay, first of all, government is never as efficient as an owner. A private owner knows better where to invest his money or the money he borrowed from a bank giving his own house as a guarantee." Eric was trying to explain something.

"Now let's say I have studied the market in the EU and I have decided that with my experience in manufacturing of wooden components for furniture, I want to invest money in Bulgaria. First, the question is, why in Bulgaria?" Eric stopped to see George and Katia's reaction. When he saw the interest in their eyes, he continued.

"A factory must be close either to its customers or to its suppliers to save on transportation costs. Remember, the market will buy the best for the least price. So the market is in the EU in general, and maybe the United States and Canada, where I have connections. Bulgaria is a very small market. The supply is beech and birch wood for furniture, and the best suppliers are in France, Germany, Romania, Finland, and the Baltic countries.

"Again, Bulgaria is a small supplier. What's left is the workforce. It must be relatively cheap and skilled and willing to work very hard. Let's say I can find that kind of employees in Bulgaria. Now I have to choose the place. It must be close to a big city, where I can find good employees. It has to be close to highways and seaports to reduce transportation costs. It has to be close to an international airport. So this sounds to me like Burgas, maybe Varna, Sofia, or Plovdiv, but not Karlovo."

"What you are saying is there is no chance for us, for small cities like Karlovo?" George asked.

"What are we supposed to do here? Do you understand how poor the people are? If not for the fact that everybody has his own garden where they grow vegetables and fruits and have animals, they would be starving. We used to have a big hospital. Now most of the doctors run to the big cities. We used to have a very good school. All the kids graduating from this school used to be accepted to universities. Now very few teachers are left. What is going to happen with us? What is going to happen with Bulgaria? Was it good for Bulgaria to be part of the EU?

"We did very well when we were close with Russia. We had a big factory with two thousand employees, producing machines for the Russian market. Then we lost the market, and the factory now has only two hundred employees. We had a factory buying all the grapes around Karlovo and making good wine, again for the Russian market. Another factory from the EU bought it, and after five years closed it to eliminate the competition. How are all these changes good for us?" George was red in the face, and the veins on his neck were pulsating.

"I'm not necessarily the one who knows all the answers," Eric said in a low voice. "In Canada I learned one thing: that sometimes you need to come out of the box to see things better. They say, 'Think outside the box!' Whatever that might mean.

"So take this from somebody outside the box." Eric continued this time with more confidence. "Karlovo's chances are for the people willing to work the land. Old people will remain; some younger people even will come back to look for the calm life of a small city. They will grow vegetables and fruits; they will look after animals. They will make their own wine and rakija, and they will be proud of it. Others will come to buy their country houses, where they will come for fun and relaxation, or where they will spend their retirement far from the busy and noisy big cities." Eric paused, expecting that everybody would agree with him.

"Sometimes I think that people like you should not be allowed to vote because you are living outside and you do not understand our problems," George suddenly said.

"Hey, I'm Bulgarian as much as you are. Do you know that we emigrants bring about $2 billion to Bulgaria every year? We help our relatives, we buy houses, and we buy furniture for the houses. We pay taxes for our properties in Bulgaria. We come here every year for our vacations, and we spend thousands of dollars in Bulgaria. I think we deserve much more respect, and actually, we have some experience that I would like to share if you are ready to open your mind ..."

"Yes, you are right. But for us, everything you say is so strange," Katia said, realizing that Eric was insulted.

"We need time to understand it," George added forcefully, in a bitter tone.

"Yes, I know. We were the same when we first arrived in Canada. Everything was different, not only the language. Now the same changes are coming to your city, your home, your life, and you do not want to accept them, but they come to you anyway. You are becoming a kind of emigrant in your own country," Eric said.

"In five to seven years, the first emigrants who left Bulgaria twenty-three years ago to live and work in the EU and America will become sixty-five years old and will start receiving their pensions from the countries they have worked in. These pensions will be enough for them to live in dignity, not in poverty as today's retired people who worked during the socialist Bulgaria.

"Preparing for retirement in Canada, the United States, and the EU is mostly a responsibility of each individual. You cannot rely just on the government. People are learning this in school, and government is teaching them how to save money for retirement. There are all kinds of tax incentives for people to take care of their own retirement and not rely only on the minimum government pension.

"As a matter of fact, that minimum is several times better than what has been inherited from the socialist regime in Bulgaria.

"One day old people in Bulgaria will receive two pensions—one Bulgarian and one much bigger from the EU. This is how it works in Canada. We receive provincial and federal (Canadian) pensions—old-age security."

This was too much for one conversation, and Eric saw that Katia and George were getting confused and tired. He let them relax and get ready for sleep. Tomorrow would be a new day. Hopefully they would be more open then, for the changes pushing their way. But they would need many more days and maybe years ... *All of us from Bulgaria need to learn more about democratic values and how to fight against the biggest enemy—corruption.*

Three days later, the vacation in Bulgaria was coming to its end. They had spent three weeks at Sunny Beach, and every day they'd gone to the sea for at least four hours.

Renee and Eric had changed their daily routine and their ideas. They somehow forgot about their own problems back in Ottawa and felt more relaxed. They were able to sleep well without any pills and despite the noise of passing cars in the street.

Every weekend they spoke with Nevena, Antony, and little Krassi. They were managing well without them. They seemed to be totally unaware of the problems and emotions in Parliament and on the streets of Sofia.

"Dad, we have our own problems; we do not have time to watch Bulgarian television on a computer," Nevena said, answering Eric's question. "Dad, Mom, next time go somewhere else. Why always Bulgaria? Go see a bit of the world."

"Yes, you are right," Renee agreed. "Next time we will buy our tickets first to Barcelona. We will spend a week there, and then we will continue to Bulgaria. The year after, we can do the same thing, but this time we will spend a week in Rome before going to Sofia."

"Good stuff," Antony agreed. "I wish we had these opportunities."

"Everything will come to its place when the time is right. Now you have to finish the university and get working. You have a family to take care of, and one more baby is on its way," Renee said. "Nevy, did you go to the doctor? Is everything okay?"

"Yes, everything is fine. We think it is a girl. It is too early to be 100 percent sure, but it looks like a girl."

"Wonderful!" Eric was excited.

"That is the best combination: a boy and a girl. I hope everything will be good … How are you doing?" he asked happily.

"I'm getting better. I'm getting fewer and fewer of these vomiting waves. Probably in a few more weeks, I will be fine. Usually in the fourth month, it stops."

They spoke a bit longer about the baby, Nevy, Antony, and how they were managing the work at the office, the studying at the university, and life at home. Then Renee asked about Maya.

"Nevena, did you talk with Maya?" Renee asked.

"Yes, Mom, She is here in Ottawa. Antony picked her up from the airport, and then she went to your home. She arrived a few days ago. Since then, she has come to see us a few times. She was happy to play with Krassi, but in a few hours, she gets bored. She is making her plans mostly with her friends."

Renee and Eric were surprised to find out that Maya changed her mind and went to Ottawa.

Renee got worried, and soon after finishing the conversation with Nevena, she called Maya on Skype.

"Maya, are you all right? What happened?" she asked.

"Everything is okay, Mom. Don't worry. I didn't tell you because I didn't want you to start worrying again.

"One of my customers has a friend who came from Ottawa, and she asked me if I could find her a furnished apartment for three weeks. I thought about it. She is a fifty-four-year-old woman and she would not damage my furniture, so I offered it to her for a thousand dollars.

"So I came home here in Ottawa with my cat, Lily."

"Don't you have any work?" Renee asked.

"Not too much. It is getting into the vacation period of the year," Maya answered and then quickly changed the subject.

"I wanted to ask you. Where is your car?"

"We suspected that you might come, so we locked it in another garage," Eric said. "You'll have to manage without a car! By the way, speak with Nevy and offer to pick up Krassi from day care. Then she might give you their car from time to time. Also, you might take one of the cats back home with you. You can help them," Eric suggested.

"Okay, I'll see. But I have rented a car. You know I can't be in Ottawa without a car.

"Do not worry about me. Tell me about you. How is your vacation?" Maya asked.

Renee was going to ask her why she was spending so much money, but Eric was quicker and changed the subject.

"It's good … but honestly, if it were not that we are Bulgarians, we wouldn't come here every year.

"There are stupid problems, like often cars don't stop when you want to cross the street. They try to scare you away, as if we are nobodies. Some drivers are driving very dangerously. Almost every day there are bad accidents on the roads and people get injured; some die.

"Cars park on the sidewalks, and people accept this as normal. Rules are broken by many, and the rest who are trying to be good citizens feel like they are being stupid. Service in the restaurants is not very good, even though I see some improvements at Sunny Beach. When I leave a good tip, as we do in Canada, my friends are asking why. They don't necessarily understand that we go to restaurants not only for the food, but for the whole experience, and getting good service and showing appreciation is part of it," Eric said.

"So go somewhere else in Western Europe. It's close from there and not expensive to travel. Why do you go every year to Bulgaria? There are so many other places you can go on vacation," Maya offered.

"No, no, we miss our country, relatives, friends, and also we are helping Bulgaria somewhat by spending our vacation money here and sharing our experience—if somebody wants to listen to us. These days everybody is willing to give advice, and people here are getting confused."

Changing the subject, Eric asked, "Have you seen the protests in Sofia?"

"Okay, Dad," Maya said, making it sound like "Please, give me a break."

"I do not watch Bulgarian television. I do not have time for that.

"I have to go now. Have a good rest of the vacation!" Maya said, smiling and waving good-bye.

Eric and Renee stayed calm and in a good mood.

Yes, the vacation was helping to calm their nerves and they were able to enjoy the company of good friends and relatives and the incredible beauty of Bulgaria. As for the rest, they were also Bulgarians, and so they understood ... As long as there were improvements every time they came, they would come again.

Before going back to Ottawa, Eric, Renee, and Nina went to see Edwin and Alexa in Sofia.

Eric wanted to ask his uncle more questions about Ovsana and her brother, Ardashes.

After the lunch Dinko and Alexa gave in their honor, Eric left Renee and Nina to talk with them, and he asked his uncle to go to the other room.

"How is Dave doing? Do you see each other?" Edwin asked.

"Yes, we keep in touch. Sometimes we go out for lunch. He is doing well," Eric answered.

"So, you have no mixed feelings anymore?" Ed asked with a smile on his face.

"Honestly, I don't. Not at all! Now I feel very comfortable with my early retirement. And also I'm sure now that Dave has been one of our good friends for the last twenty-two years," Eric said.

"I'm glad to hear this. Stay friends with him and his family!" Uncle Ed said this with a voice only an older person can use to his younger relatives.

"How is your book coming along?" his uncle asked with interest.

"Well, I'm advancing. Now it is coming much easier than before. I cannot explain why. I'm hoping to have it finished this fall, and maybe for Christmas I can send you the book as a gift." Eric was smiling. "I hope you will like it."

"I'm sure it will be good. You remind me of an Armenian writer from California. I will not say his name. You have a similar style," his uncle said.

"What are you going to do after you finish with this book? Maybe you can write another one," Ed was smiling, trying to encourage him again.

"Thank you, Uncle Ed. You have helped me a lot. You gave me so much confidence, but let me finish this one first. I'm not sure yet how I'm going to end it," Eric said.

"You don't have to. That way you will start writing your next book." Ed was now laughing.

"Uncle Ed, I want to ask you about your grandmother, Ovsana." Eric drew his attention back to his grandmother.

"I do not understand why Ovsana did not get married after Grandma Arakssi got married. She was only thirty-one years old."

"Well, nobody would marry a woman with a sick child. Her son, Hagop, became very sick. You know, he barely survived meningitis when he was five years old. He was not able to recover completely. He grew up as a mentally retarded man," his uncle said.

"I didn't know that. I remember him as an old man who from time to time came home to see us. He was very slim. His cheekbones stuck out on his unshaven face. He brought us kids Turkish bagels. I do not know much of him. We never spoke with him. He always went straight to see our grandmother, Arakssi."

"Yes, he got sick when Ovsana was working at the military hospital in Plovdiv during the First World War. Most probably he got infected from a virus carried home from the hospital. Ovsana stopped working in the hospital. She was afraid to bring other diseases home to her kids," his uncle said.

"But then how did she manage taking care of her family? It must have been very difficult," Eric said.

"It was difficult for everybody during the war. She worked at the homes of Armenian families. She cooked and cleaned for them."

Uncle Ed tried to remember more, but he couldn't. "I do not remember much about her stories for this period of her life; most probably she didn't want to talk about this."

"But then how did you know that our great-uncle Ardashes died in 1919 in East Turkey?" Eric asked.

"There was a Bulgarian officer I knew about from my grandmother who used to be a friend to Ardashes. After the war, he came to see Ovsana, and he helped the family as he had apparently promised our granduncle. My mother told us that he liked Ovsana. He came to see her and her kids. He helped them with whatever he could in these hungry years right after the war. Most probably he told her about the end of Ardashes."

They continued talking about Ovsana, Arakssi and Ardashes and then Edwin brought an old box with many picture of his mother and grandmother. There on the bottom Eric saw a bundle of old letters. Some were written in Armenian and some in Turkish. These letters were written in old Turkish form of Arabic script. They couldn't read it. Modern Turkish is based on Latin letters and was introduced only in the beginning of 1929 from Kemal Ataturk, the father of modern Turkey.

Eric asked his uncle if he can take these letters with him and find somebody to translate them.

May 1919

Ovsana was waiting for Methody to come.

Since the end of the war, he came regularly every weekend on Sundays for a cup of coffee and some cakes at her house. He brought small presents to the kids, some bread, cheese, and sometimes meat for the family.

More than a year had passed since he came the last time, though. She didn't really expect to see him anymore.

"Ovsana, do you remember me?" he asked her when she opened the door for him.

He had grown up and become a serious man in his late thirties. He had a few scars on his face, he limped as he walked, and he was holding a cane in his left hand.

"Yes, I do …" was the only thing she was able to say before she hugged him as if he were a family member. Then she quickly stepped back, and her face became red.

"I was not expecting to see you, Lieutenant Terziev. How are you? Please come in." She opened the door wider.

"I'm sorry, Ovsana. I was not able to come and see you earlier, as I promised. I was caught in the war far away from here." He was smiling with his face and eyes.

"But now that I'm back, I will come more often if you don't mind. I promised your brother to help you, and I will help you if you allow me."

"Lieutenant Terziev, you do not have to do anything for us. I'm just happy to see you alive." Ovsana was also smiling.

"Please, call me Metho, as my friends do. The war is over, and now I'm a civilian. I'm retired from the army, and I just came back from the hospital.

"How are the kids? How have you gone through the war? It must have been very difficult for a single mother with two kids," he asked.

Ovsana cried while explaining the difficulties she had after her son became sick from meningitis. She blamed herself as the reason he got this virus.

"I was working at the hospital with so many injured and sick solders. I might have brought home this virus to my son. It was terrible. He survived, but his mental ability is not the same anymore." She was crying.

"He is now nine years old, but mentally he is like five years old. He doesn't go to school. He wants to stay next to me all the time. He is a good boy, but he is not growing up normally as the other boys his age." Ovsana was sobbing in pain.

"He will be all right with time. I'm sure he will improve." Metho was trying to calm her down.

"How is your daughter?" he asked.

"Thank God, she is doing very well. Arakssi is now thirteen years old. She is smart, and she loves studying. She is growing into a beautiful young woman." Now the shadows of pain left her face.

Ovsana and Metho had a lot to talk about—both themselves and what had happened for the last five years during the war.

She found out that he had lost his family during the war. He was alone, and he avoided talking about that.

She asked whether he had any news about Ardashes. He said that the last time he saw him was the same night when they met for the first time. He was supposed to go to East Turkey and fight there for the liberation of Armenia on the side of the Russian Army under the command of General Antranik. He promised to ask his friends to see if somebody had any news about Arda and the other Armenians from General Antranik's army. He did not know anything new. The only thing he knew was that General Antranik was still fighting on the east border of Turkey, protecting the independence of the new Armenian state.

"I will come next Sunday again if you don't mind," Metho said, and he stood up. "I would like to see your kids," he said while walking to the door.

"I will look forward to seeing you next Sunday," Ovsana said happily. The war and the tough life had taught them to accept the good moments and not pretend that it was not important for them. They

215

both were happy they met again and did not hide it.

As time passed, Ovsana and Metho remained friends. One day in July 1919, he came with news about her brother, Ardashes.

"Ovsana, finally I found somebody who actually was with your brother during the war in East Turkey. I met him in the Armenian club. I first learned about him from my Macedonian friends. They had fought together during the 1913 war against Turkey. He told me he saw his Armenian friend in a pub in the old city of Plovdiv." Metho started relating the story he had been told.

"Is Ardashes alive?" Ovsana interrupted him impatiently.

"Let me tell you what I discovered, and you decide for yourself," Metho said.

"Aram was drunk when I met him, but he remembered Ardashes and he was willing to talk to me." Metho began telling her their conversation.

Metho said, "Aram, I know you through my friends from the Balkan War. I was also participating, and we fought side by side with Ardashes. Do you know him?"

"Yes, I do." Aram picked up his eyes to better see the tall Bulgarian man who was standing next to his table.

"Can I sit?" Metho asked him, hanging his cane on the back of a chair.

Aram didn't answer; he just made a gesture to the empty chair beside him.

"Why are you drinking so much?" Metho asked him.

Aram ignored his question and kept on looking at Metho.

"Yes, I know you. I've seen you with Arda during 1913. It was a great victory when we took Edirne," Aram said with flames in his eyes.

"But now everything is forgotten … I'm an emigrant here in this country, and nobody pays attention to me …" His head dropped again, and he started looking at his empty cup on the table.

"I came back to Bulgaria to look for my family, but I couldn't find them. I do not know where they are. Some people said they went to America; some said they died, but I do not know where their graves are."

"Yes, we all have our stories," Metho said. "I lost my family also. Nobody has seen them, and nobody knows if they are alive or dead.

"I still have hope, and I have asked the Red Cross to look for them. The war has separated so many people. Do not lose your hope!" Metho said.

Aram looked up again in his eyes.

"I hope you are right, my friend. Why are you asking me about Arda?" Aram asked, now completely taking control over himself.

"Because he is a dear friend and also because he has family here in Plovdiv and they need to know what happened to him," Metho said emotionally.

"Ardashes died fighting for the lives of the Armenians from Van," Aram said

"What happened, though? How did he die?" Metho kept on asking Aram to get more details.

"It was the spring of 1918, when the Russian army started withdrawing from the liberated West Armenia in the district of Van in East Turkey. After the Bolshevik revolution in Russia in October 1917, the monarchy was brought down. The new communist government of Russia quickly signed a peace treaty with Turkey in March 1918. According to the treaty, West Armenia would remain part of Turkey and East Armenia was part of the Russian Federation.

"We were left alone in East Turkey with only a few thousand Armenian volunteers and two hundred officers under the command of General Antranik and some Russian officers who volunteered to protect the Armenian civilian population. The Russian Army disintegrated, leaving most of their ammunition to the Armenian volunteers. We had to stop the regular Turkish Army from advancing. They wanted to block all the ways for the Armenian population of West Armenia to escape to East Armenia, which was part of the Russian Federation." Aram was explaining the situation at that time in East Turkey.

"There was no chance for us to stop them taking Van. They were three times more numerous than us. We were afraid that the civilians might be killed so Turkey could avoid future wars and demands from Armenia and Russia. Our hope was to evacuate them and protect the narrow roads and paths in the high passes through the surrounding mountains. This would give time for the slowly moving tens of thousands of civilians to go behind the new positions of the Armenian Volunteer Army. Here we could stop the advancing of a much bigger Turkish military force." Aram's expression had changed, and his black eyes were illuminating his scarred and unshaven face.

"Ardashes was injured in his leg, and he decided with a few other friends to stay and fight. They were not able to walk fast because of their wounds, so they took an elevated position over the passage cliff, behind rocks and boulders. He kept with him plenty of ammunition and told us that they would try to stop the advancing of the Turkish soldiers and the irregular Kurds for as long as they could last.

"The narrow road twisted like a snake right below him. On one side was the almost vertical wall of the mountain slope, and on the other side was the open space between the two slopes of the mountain ridges. Somewhere a hundred meters down in the bottom, the two slopes joined at the river. There was no other way around for at least fifty kilometers, so the advancing army had to go through this high mountain passage." Aram explained the details of the position Arda and his friends took for their last fight.

"Arda was a very good shot. I'm sure he did not let anybody pass during the time his rifle was cracking. We heard the noise of the shooting for more than two hours." Aram stopped talking, and his eyes were now full of tears.

"They were good friends …" he managed to say.

"Yes, they were …" Metho agreed, wiping his own moisture from his nose.

He stood up. He held his cane as if he were holding his rifle and walked out without limping.

This was bad news for Ovsana, and she took it very hard. But she was somehow not surprised. She knew Arda would risk his life to save the lives of others.

She was proud of him. She would never forget him and what he did for so many people, saving their lives and helping them have their own country. He succeeded. East Armenia remained out of the Ottoman Empire. Arda was not alive to see it and enjoy it himself.

But is he really dead? Nobody saw him die. Maybe he escaped somehow. Ovsana was not sure; she still had a small hope that he might be alive somewhere in the mountains of East Turkey.

Metho kept on coming every Sunday and was able to slowly change her mind; she started looking positively again on the world around her.

October 1923

Ovsana was waiting for Metho to come for the last time.

She was seated at home and was thinking about how many things had changed in her life just in the last few months.

In the beginning of the summer, Arakssi got married to Agop and moved out with her husband. Ovsana felt so relaxed. Finally there was a man in her family who would take care of Arakssi and hopefully could help her and her son. In few months, Arakssi got pregnant, and Ovsana couldn't stop smiling. She was going to have a grandchild.

Ovsana was full with her own hopes for a better life for herself as well. She was hiding deep in her heart the small hope that maybe one day Metho would ask her to get married. They understood each other well, and they were so happy talking together. He was always available

if she needed help. But again, this
was too much to hope for. She was not
free. She had her son who had mental
problems. He was now thirteen years old,
but behaved like an eight-year-old. She
had to spend a lot of time with him, and
maybe this would be acceptable to Metho.
She quickly tried to wave away her empty
hopes.

*Why did he send me a letter saying
that this Sunday he would come to my
house for the last time?* Ovsana was
worried.

What did he mean by this? she wondered.

*Something has happened, and he will
no longer be able to come and see me.*
Ovsana didn't know what to think.

The last few nights she couldn't sleep
well. She would wake up seeing Metho
going away in a boat.

When she opened the door, Metho was
standing there looking down at his feet.
His face was serious, and Ovsana felt
she would faint.

"What happened ...?" was all she could
ask while stepping back into the room.

"Ovsana, I came here to tell you
this myself. I was thinking of sending

you a letter, but that was not right …" Metho was speaking in a low voice, still holding his head down.

"Do you remember? I wrote many letters to the Red Cross looking for my wife and son." Now he looked in her eyes.

"After so many years, my hope was becoming slim. I was not thinking that it could be possible to find them. Last week I received a letter from the Red Cross. They found them. They are alive …" His voice started to crack, and tears streamed down his face.

Ovsana was stunned. She was not expecting this. She was standing in the middle of the room and still not realizing what was going on.

"Ovsana, they are alive, and they are waiting for me in Chicago, America," Metho said, now smiling through his tears.

Finally Ovsana reacted. She came close to him and hugged him.

"I'm happy for you, Metho. You deserve to be happy and with your family. This is a miracle. How did they survive, and what they are doing so far away in

America?" She could speak now, completely overcoming her first emotions.

"I received a letter from my wife, Marisa, and my son, Stefan. He is now twelve years old, and he can speak Bulgarian and English as well." Metho was smiling happily.

"He wrote me in Bulgarian. 'Dad, come home. I'm waiting for you ...' My wife explained in her letter how a Greek military boat took them from the coast when their village was burned down. First they spent a year on the Greek island of Rhodes in a Red Cross camp, and then an American boat took them to New York. They stayed there about a year before they discovered that there was a bigger Bulgarian and Macedonian community in Chicago. With other Bulgarian emigrants, they moved there."

Metho was explaining to Ovsana how his family ended up living in Chicago. He carefully looked into her eyes and tried to see if she were disappointed.

Ovsana forced a smile on her face, but her heart was hurting and something was holding her throat. She tried to speak, but she couldn't. Her mouth stayed open while she looked in his eyes.

"Ovsana, I must go to them. You understand, this is my family. Every night I've been asking God for my wife and son to be alive and to find them. I know this will be hard for you. We got close … and I do not know what to say." Metho was looking for the right words.

"You do not have to say anything more. You've been here for me and my family for the last five years … I will miss you … My son will miss you …" Ovsana turned her head so he could not see her tears.

"Ovsana, why don't you come with your son to Chicago? I will be able to help you there. Your daughter is married now, and she lives with her husband. I'm sure your son would have better conditions in America." Metho asked this impulsively out of his own emotions.

"No, no, I can't do that. My daughter will soon have a child, and she is still a child herself. I have to be here for them. And what would you say to your wife? No, no, this is impossible. You go. I will stay here with my family." Ovsana was now very sure of herself.

"I will miss you also …" Metho said and kissed her good-bye. "I will send you my address when I settle in Chicago. Write me if you need something. I will help you from there …"

"Go now!" Ovsana managed to say while fighting her tears with wrinkles between her eyebrows.

Metho slowly left, leaving the door open and his cane forgotten on the back of a chair.

August 2013

Eric and Renee came back from vacation well relaxed and full of energy. They were impatient to see their grandson, Krassi, their daughters, Maya and Nevena, as well as Nevena's husband, Antony. They were all together again in Ottawa, and everybody was happy.

They had not forgotten Nikola, and the first day after returning, Nina, Renee, and Eric visited Nikola's grave and placed fresh flowers on it. Nina opened a small plastic bag and took out a handful of earth from the garden of their house, where they had lived together for more than forty years.

Eric was about to say that she didn't have the right to do that, but he just bit his tongue.

This was part of the land that they had left in Europe. Nikola was here to stay on this new land in Canada forever. Canada was no more a foreign land for them. It was the land where the grave of their father and grandfather was.

In few days, Eric started working on his project to build a pergola in the backyard of their house, and Renee started picking up Krassi from day care.

Eric had already designed all the parts of the pergola with the help of special engineering software called SolidWorks. He had assembled them in a final SolidWorks drawing, and now he was ready to order all the material. He was excited to start actually making all the parts in red cedar, painting them with a special European transparent wood finish and then assembling the pergola on their deck. This pergola had to be something really nice.

Before going on vacation, Eric researched existing designs and what materials he could use. He discussed it with Renee, and then he started designing their own pergola, taking elements they liked from several other designs. In the beginning, he was not sure he could make it, but once he started working, everything came out as planned. He was enjoying what he was doing and was not rushing it. He worked from 8:00 a.m. to about 3:00 p.m. It took him two full weeks, including the weekends, to completely finish it. Renee helped him, holding the other end of the long parts so he could bolt or screw them together. It became strong and beautiful.

While working on the pergola, Eric thought about the book and was writing notes when Renee went to pick up their grandchild. His writing was going faster and easier now, and he started enjoying it also. He was now doing things he liked, and hopefully others would like them also.

When the pergola was complete, the neighbors came to say how much they liked it.

"It is good not only for you, but for us as well as a decoration of our backyard," one of their neighbors said.

"Bravo. Good work. Enjoy it!" another neighbor said.

"I'm sorry for the noise and the dust during the last two weeks. Please come over for a drink." Eric and Renee invited them.

Eric was happy, and Renee was proud.

Maya, when she returned to Victoria, followed the development of the pergola on Skype every day. When it was ready, she gave her thumbs-up. "Dad, if you came here to Victoria, you could make $10,000 per pergola."

"I doubt somebody would pay so much, but thank you. I understand what you mean." Eric started laughing.

The same weekend, Nevy, Antony, and Krassi came for dinner. They stayed outside on the deck under the pergola.

"Wow, Dad. This is really great. I didn't know you were such a good carpenter. Your yard is certainly now the best-looking in the neighborhood." Nevy didn't stop complimenting him.

"Thank you, Nevy. Your mom helped me in both the design and the actual work on this project. We have always been a good team," Eric said while kissing his wife.

The happiest of all was Krassi. He was so overexcited with the attention of his grandparents; he was now making noises like a tiger, trying to scare them. They all laughed, but the cat got really scared and ran inside the house.

Eric looked at his daughter and thought, *Why did she put Krassi in an Armenian kindergarten? She doesn't know Armenian. I'm half Armenian and half Bulgarian, Renee is Bulgarian, and Antony is Bulgarian. Whatever the reason was, I'm happy,* Eric thought. *And little Krassi seems to be happy as well.*

Eric hugged his grandson and kissed him on the top of his head.

"I love you, Dedi Eri ..." Little Krassi said in English, lifting up his head.

"I love you too." Eric was smiling, and so was Nevy.

As the summer got closer to its end, the days were cooler in the mornings and warm in the afternoons.

Now is the time to concentrate on the book, Eric thought. He was afraid that he would not be able to pull all these stories together into one interesting novel.

"What is it, Eric?" Renee asked him one day while she was preparing dinner. "You appear to be concerned about something."

"Yes, it is the book. I'm afraid I'm not going to make it. So many people will read it, and they might laugh at me," Eric said

"It is not the time to give up," Renee said angrily. "You already told everybody we know that you are working on it. They will laugh at you if you don't do it. Why did you contact the publishing house last week? You already paid them part of the money to publish it.

"Actually, I know why you did it. All this talking with all your friends and relatives for the last two years ..." Renee looked at Eric with her hands on her hips.

"Yes, I know I promised to do it, so I have to do it." Eric was now smiling.

"Yes, that's why you did all that, so you could not give up," she added.

"But I'm still afraid."

"No, you are not afraid. You are just concerned whether you can write something good. If not, you will just be wasting our money and your time to fulfill your promises to your grandparents and now to everybody else around us." Renee was putting the events in order.

Then she smiled and said, "Do not worry. You will do well. I'm sure of it. Your kids told you the same thing. Your uncle Ed said he liked your style of writing. I liked it as well." Renee kept helping him get his confidence back.

"Okay. I'm sure tomorrow I will feel better about it," Eric said, still not sounding very convinced.

"Let's eat now. Tomorrow is another day." Renee brought the plates to the table.

April 1918

Ardashes was now alone, hidden behind
the rocks and boulders, stuck about ten
meters over the road. His two friends
were no longer alive. They took too
long to aim with their rifles, and they
allowed themselves to be exposed for
too long. The Turkish soldiers took them
down in the first fifteen minutes.

Arda had a different style. He did not
lift his head to find targets. The road
stretched down about a hundred meters
before disappearing behind a mountain
cliff. The Turks and Kurds were hiding
behind it. If they decided to run to
his position, they had to run a hundred
meters before they could reach cover.
Arda had a small mirror in his pocket.
He took it out and carefully adjusted it
against a rock with the correct angle to
see the road and the cliff.

He sat there and watched for somebody to lose his patience and come out from behind the cliff. He had about ten meters of space in his rocky nest, and he would move to different positions every time he decided to shoot. He appeared for just a second, and when he shot his rifle, he always hit the target. He had not missed a single shot.

The Kurds were angry every time he appeared for a second and shouted loudly at him. The-well trained regular Turkish soldiers preferred to stay hidden and aim for the rocky nest from their hidden positions.

Arda knew what they were waiting for. They were waiting to bring up artillery. Against it he had no chance, but for now, he had the upper hand, and he was holding them down, gaining time for the civilians to move away as far as possible. Then his friends from the Armenian Volunteer Army would make another ambush and again stop the advance of the Turkish Army.

His leg was hurting him, but he had stopped the blood from the wound and for now it was not a problem. He was an experienced soldier, and then he became a young officer in the army of General Antranik after his first battles during the Balkan War in 1912. He had been at war for almost seven years. He was now twenty-eight years old and already a veteran of the Armenian Volunteer Army. He knew what to do, and he knew when he could not do anything else but withdraw.

He kept them pinned down behind a cliff on the far side of the road for about two hours before he finally saw the heavy gun coming out and slowly aiming at his position. He had only ten to fifteen seconds before they fired.

Arda had prepared for that. He had taken with him only things he needed. He kept his pistol, and he put in his pockets enough bullets for it. He had his dagger, some dry meat, and a metal bottle with water—a gift from a Russian soldier. He had prepared a rope with the long cloth belts of his fallen friends and had attached it on the other side of his position when he planned his escape. When he saw the neck of the big gun turning toward him, he left his rifle and moved swiftly out of the nest from the back side, where the rope was hanging.

He had managed to come only halfway down when the rocks above his head burst out in all directions. And then he heard the roar of the cannon. Small stones and dust came down around him, but he was safe. In five more seconds, he was down on the road on the hidden side of the mountain cliff.

He had no chances remaining on the road. He couldn't run, and for sure the Kurds had come with their horses. They would kill him in just a minute or two. They were definitely already running to his position and would be there within twenty seconds. Arda made the sign of the cross with his right hand, touching his forehead, and then he jumped off the road down the slope. He kept his legs together and his arms around his head—and disappeared …

He fell straight down about fifteen meters before his legs, and then his bottom and back, reached the slope covered with thousands of small stones. He slid with them down for about fifty meters till he reached the end of the next cliff. Before going farther down, he heard the second roar of the cannon somewhere far above him where the road was. He fell another ten to fifteen meters. Again he landed on a steep slope and started sliding down on the small stones around him.

He was coming close to the bottom because the angle of the slope was decreasing and there were now bushes between the stones. He tried slowing down by grabbing the bushes, and finally he reached the bottom, where big stones and boulders had piled up. Between them ran a mountain river, coming down from the high peaks still covered with snow. Tall trees grew on both sides, hiding the river.

He checked himself. His adrenalin was high, and he did not feel any pain. To be sure he was okay, he started moving his legs and arms one by one. Once he had checked that all his limbs worked, he stood and looked up the slope. He couldn't believe where he had come from. It was impossible to see the road, and surely nobody could see him. He doubted if anybody had seen him jump down; and even if they did, who would come after him? In any case, he moved closer to the river below the trees.

He started slowly moving downstream, walking around big boulders that had fallen there maybe centuries earlier. In some places there was still snow not completely melted. He avoided them, leaving no tracks. It was difficult to keep going, but he pushed himself, trying to go as far as possible from the place he fell.

That was why he remained alive—he was smart and didn't take chances. He never underestimated his enemy. He knew the Turkish officers were smart and capable. Somebody would remember him jumping down and could send soldiers with long ropes down to look for him. The chance was small, but it kept him going for hours.

The night deep in the valley was coming much faster, so he had to find shelter. Nights in the mountains were cold and long. He started looking for dry bushes, dry branches, and old grass to make a nest so he would not be lying on the cold ground. He found a place well-hidden below a big rock, just in case it rained.

He made it bigger and wider so he could go inside.

Suddenly a violent rain began. He wrapped himself with his pelerine and put the hood on his head. Holding the handle of his dagger, he fell asleep. He was exhausted, and he needed a rest for his body and his injured leg. Just before falling asleep, he heard crackling from rifles coming from far away.

They reached the second ambush, he thought to himself. *Please, God, save the Armenians.*

Arda had slept for about four hours when the rain stopped as suddenly as it had started. It became cold and humid. He was dry under the rock in his nest of branches and dry grass, but he started thinking about the children and women and elderly people who were now somewhere in the mountains running for their lives.

"Why are the Armenians suffering so much? Why are you letting so many innocent people perish?" he asked God.

"We just want our freedom and independence like all other Christian nations under the Ottoman rule. It looks like the rest of the world has forgotten us.

"Please, God, help us!" By now Arda was praying loudly.

Suddenly he heard some noise unusual for this place. He concentrated to understand what it was and where it was coming from.

A child was crying.

"That is impossible. What is a child doing here?" Arda asked loudly.

He went from his shelter and started walking slowly in the direction of the crying child. It was dark, but at least it was no longer raining.

Now he could hear people talking in low voices. It was Armenian. He came closely as carefully as he could without making too much noise.

"*Mi goular manchas! Mi goular!* Do not cry, my boy! Don't!" A woman held a small boy in her arms, and next to her stood a bigger child. The clouds had cleared and some light from the moon was shining through, just enough to see the shapes of a seated woman with two children.

"Do not be afraid," Arda said in a low voice. "I'm an Armenian as well." He slowly came out from behind a rock.

"You are all wet. Come with me. I have a dry shelter not far from here." Arda was speaking in Armenian. He took off his pelerine and gave it to the woman.

"Take this; you will need it." Arda was trying to help them.

They were shaking from cold, and their clothes were all wet.

"Let me help you," he said, now touching her hand.

She took his hand and the pelerine. Then she put her son on the ground next to her daughter and wrapped them together with it. Then she turned back to Arda.

"Who are you? What are you doing here?" she asked.

"I'm hiding here and trying to go to East Armenia. Let me take you to the shelter first. We can talk afterward." He picked up both kids and asked her to walk after him.

In a few minutes, they were in front of his improvised bed below a big boulder.

"Go inside, the three of you. I will stay out here and protect you." The day before, he had seen coyotes eating from dead bodies thrown down from the road above.

They listened to him and went inside.

"Take off your clothes. They are all soaked in water, and you will get sick. I will dry them here on the branches of a tree with the wind." He was talking as a father would to his kids.

She listened to him, and then she hugged her two kids and tried to get them warm with her body and the pelerine. They were so tired that soon after, she and her two kids fell asleep.

The sun was slowly coming down to the top of the trees. Arda had hung their clothes on the lower branches. Warm spring wind was rapidly drying them.

Arda checked again on the woman with the two kids. They were still sleeping, but it was time to wake them up. He put their clothes in front of them on the dry branches in the shelter and walked away, making a little noise with his feet.

"How did you come here? What is your name?" Arda asked the woman when they joined him on the bank of the river.

"I'm Navart, and these are my children, Nigohos and Siranush," she said, looking at him.

"My father's name was Nigohos," Arda said, picking up the small boy.

"How did you come here?" he again asked Navart.

"My husband was killed during the siege of Van in 1915," she said. "Turks and Kurds were killing the Armenians in the villages. They were entering their houses under the pretext of searching for Russian rifles. Armenians who escaped ran to Van for protection. The Turkish army surrounded Van. We were about one hundred thousand Armenians living in Van, and there were only about a thousand Armenians with rifles and pistols to protect us against five thousand Turkish soldiers and Kurds. They wanted to massacre us all. We were saved by the Russian Army." Navart told him her story.

"Yes, I came with the Armenian Volunteer Army of Antranik Pasha, together with the Russian Army, to free Van," Arda told her, still holding Nigohos in his hands.

Navart continued, "I lived with my father and the children in Van for three years. But then the Russian Army decided to withdraw, and we were left under the protection of only a few thousand Armenian soldiers of General Antranik. When we learned that the Turkish Army and a few thousand irregular Kurds were coming, we were afraid. We ran from the city with other civilian Armenians to East Armenia in Russian territory looking for the Russian soldiers. We thought they would wait for us and protect us. We moved slowly, and we were left alone without protection. Kurds attacked us on the road, killing the men, raping the women, and stealing the children." She was shaking in horror.

"It was terrible," she said simply. "They killed my father in front of my eyes, and they were coming for me and my kids. I do not know how, but I just grabbed my kids and jumped off the road, hoping for a miracle.

"We fell down and down and I thought it was the end, but then we reached the slope below the cliff. We started sliding together with the small stones accumulated on the slope till we came to the very bottom, next to the river. We were alive. I couldn't believe it. We started slowly moving down the river. Two days later, we met you." She was now crying, remembering again what she had seen and what she had to go through.

"And you. How did you come here? Who are you?" She asked him.

Arda told her that he was from the Armenian Volunteer Army of General Antranik. He told her that they were retreating at the rear of forty thousand civilians from Van heading to East Armenia. He told her how the Armenian soldiers were making ambushes to slow down the advancing Turkish soldiers and the Kurds. He told her his story of how he had jumped when there was nothing else he could do. He saved her the details of the fights. He skipped talking about the hundreds of dead Armenian bodies he saw upriver. Coyotes were feasting on them, not paying any attention to him.

"You must be hungry. When was the last time you ate?" he asked them. Then he offered Navart and the kids some of the dry meat he had and water from his bottle.

For more than twenty days, they walked slowly during the day along the river around big stones, trees, and bushes, making their way down the narrow river valley. Arda caught crabs behind the stones in the river and sometimes small fish. They had to eat them raw. He was afraid of making fires that might be seen from the road. He was sure Kurds were still controlling the area and trying to catch any fleeing Armenians.

At night, they slept in shelters they prepared together, putting the kids between them. Arda had changed. He had had enough of the war. What had it brought them? There were two peace treaties he knew about. The first one was in 1913 between Bulgaria, Serbia, and Greece on one side and Turkey on the other side. The second one was between Bolshevik Russia and Turkey in March 1918 after four years of war. In both treaties, Armenians in Turkey were left on their own.

He had participated in all the wars against Turkey with the hope Armenians from East Turkey would achieve their independence. But this didn't bring freedom to them. Left alone to fight against the angry Turks and Kurds, they now had to fight to save the lives of the civilian Armenian population. He participated in the last battles to protect the Armenians running out from the city of Van. His comrades from the Volunteer Army were continuing the battles, and hopefully they would be able to save part of the civilian population from extermination.

Arda now had his own small battle. He wanted to protect that Armenian woman with her two small children. He wanted to save them and take them out of Turkey. He felt something new. He felt an attachment to Navart and her small kids. Nigohos, three years old, was not crying anymore. He was holding Arda's hand while walking, or picking up his two hands when he was tired, asking Arda to carry him. Siranush, five years old, was shy, but she did not leave his side. Navart's face was now lightened by her new hope, and her big eyes did not miss any of Arda's motions. She was a beautiful young mother in her early twenties, and Arda was attracted to her beauty and innocence.

They were coming close to an area where the narrow valley of the small river they had followed for three weeks started opening to a wider valley, where the river was joining the bigger Aras (Araks) River. The Aras ran along the border territories of Turkey, Northern Iran, East Armenia, and Azerbaijan. The slopes on both sides of the valley were lessening; they were not so high and steep. Arda was getting worried. It was getting easier for the Kurds to come down with their horses and check the small riverbanks for escaping Armenians.

"Navart, you have to stay here and wait for me. I have to find out the positions of our Armenian Volunteer Army. They should be here somewhere. I'm going to scout the area before we continue. There might be Kurds sitting in ambush. Wait for me and do not worry. I might not come back for a day or two." He left the shelter early in the morning, a few hours before daybreak.

The whole day and night passed. Navart didn't know what to think or what to expect. She was worried and couldn't sleep.

Just about daybreak on the following morning, she heard three quick shots and the noise of scared birds fleeing the trees.

Just thirty minutes later, she saw Arda coming back down the slope with three horses and four small Armenian kids riding them.

"We have to leave now," Arda said in a hurry. "We are very close to East Armenia and our army positions. I'm afraid there will be more Kurds and maybe Turkish regular soldiers in the area. Can you ride?" he asked her.

"Yes, my father taught me." she answered, holding back her questions about what had happened and how he got these Armenian kids.

"You have to rush! We have no time," Arda said urgently, holding one of the horses for her.

She mounted it as men do, and she put her boy in front of her and the girl behind her. Arda did the same with two small kids; he put the other two, bigger boys on the third horse. He roped the horse with the two boys to his horse, and without losing any more time, he headed to the wide valley in front of them. The Armenian kids were scared, but Navart was speaking to them all the time in Armenian, trying to calm them and make them feel safe.

The road was now visible on their right side coming down to the valley, which was opening wider. Once they reached the road, he forced the horses to gallop toward the Russian Federation border. It was not far anymore. They could see the positions of the Armenian soldiers about two kilometers from them.

"Please, God, let us pass the border." Arda was praying loudly, constantly turning his head and looking for any Kurds. The border was now only about six or seven hundred meters away. Arda looked back again, and he saw five horsemen galloping wildly about two hundred meters behind them.

Arda slowed his horse and gave the reins to Navart. If he pushed the horses at full gallop, the kids would fall off.

"Continue. Do not stop; go straight to the barracks," he shouted at her as he jumped from the horse.

He looked around for something to hide behind. Suddenly he felt a pain below his left shoulder, and then he heard the rifles of the Kurds. The shot made him turn and pushed him down to the ground in the middle of the road. He lay on his face, his legs toward the coming horsemen. They were coming in at full gallop. He didn't move. He didn't even raise his head to see where they were; instead, he pretended to be dead. He was tempted to reach for his pistol, but he didn't.

He waited for them to come close. When they were almost next to him, he quickly turned on his back, pulled out his pistol, and fired five shots. Three of the horses continued galloping without their riders, trying to reach the other two horses in front of them. The other two had stopped a few meters away, forced by the reins attached around the arms of their fallen riders.

Arda stood up and mounted one of the horses; he cut the reins of the other horses, and gathered all of them together. He galloped to the Armenian border, where solders were waiting for them.

A Russian officer was looking at him with admiration. He spoke in Armenian with a Russian accent.

"Welcome to the Russian Federation. Here you will be safe. Who are this woman and these kids?"

"This is my family," Arda said.

The officer looked again at Navart and the six kids, and he said smiling, "You have a young woman and already with 6 kids."

"Yes, we married early," Arda answered, while Navart was looking at him with an open mouth.

"Who are you?" the officer asked, looking now at his uniform as an officer from the Armenian Volunteer Army and his pistol and dagger stuck in his belt. Arda did not want to say who he was.

"He is my husband, Vartan. We were living in Van before the Turks and the Kurds came after us, trying to kill all the Armenians," Navart answered for him.

"Yes, we know what is going on. We have tens of thousands of refugees in our camps. They told us about all the horrible things the Turks and the Kurds were doing to the civilian Armenian population. They are practically exterminating them from their homelands," the Russian officer said angrily.

"Here in the Russian Federation, we have had our own Armenian Christian population for centuries; they are well respected by the law and by the Russian people," he said.

Then to explain his decent Armenian, he told them his name. "My name is Viktor Gregorian. My father is Armenian, and my mother is Russian."

Then he turned again to Arda, smiling with his eyes. "Not bad for a civilian. Where did you find this uniform and the horses?"

"Some Kurds gave them to me."

"Yes, I saw everything from here. They were rushing after you …" He was smiling. "What are you going to do with the horses?" he asked Arda.

"I will sell them. Do you want them?" Arda asked.

"Yes. What do you want for them?"

"Give us new clothes for me and my family, food, medications," Arda said. "They will be yours after we reach the refugee camp, and also I want a separate home for my family," Arda added.

Now the officer was laughing loudly.

"Yes, I can see you are an Armenian. Okay, I will try doing that for you. Welcome again to the Russian Federation. We like brave men." He looked at Arda's wounded shoulder and the blood dripping from his leg. You are injured."

He turned to a lower-ranking officer and said something in Russian.

He helped Arda, Navart, and the kids to dismount from the horses and invited them into the barracks.

They were accepted into a refugee camp in East Armenia with thousands of Armenians from East Turkey.

Arda had complications with his injured leg.

"The wound in the leg has been neglected for a long time," a Russian Army doctor said. "We have to operate and clean out all the infection. The wound in the shoulder is clean, and it will slowly close with time," he added after checking it carefully.

Two days after the operation, the same doctor came again to check his leg.

"I have to open the wound and clean it out again to prevent gangrene. There is a danger we will have to cut your leg off," the doctor said.

Arda said nothing while the doctor cut his wound open again and removed some infected flesh. The doctor closed it carefully and looked at Navart.

"You have to change his bandages every day and put fresh medication on it from what I'm going to give you. It should be fine."

"Why are you doing all this, coming from the city all the way up here in the camp to operate on my husband?" Navart asked the doctor.

The doctor smiled. "This is my job, and also your husband sold his horses to the Russian Officers Army."

"But how come?" she asked again, surprised.

"Well, a friend of mine, Viktor, told me he bought eight horses from you," the doctor said and left their tent.

Arda was smiling under his long mustache.

"He could have taken those horses from us anyway," Navart said.

"No, an honest officer would never do that. He could not steal from refugees." Arda was still smiling.

A week passed.

Navart was now always close to Arda, helping and changing the bandages and applying medication for his wounds. Slowly the infection disappeared.

In May, Viktor moved them to an Armenian house in a village in Georgia about 150 kilometers northwest from the place they entered East Armenia.

"Here you will be safer than in East Armenia, far from the border with Turkey," Viktor explained to them.

"East Armenia declared independence from the Russian Federation. I'm afraid the Turkish Army will come against

Armenia. It will be an easier target for them without the protection of the Russian Federation.

"For us, the Russian officers from the ex-Russian Federation of Czar Nicholas Romanov, there is no place in Armenia and no reason to stay," Viktor added. "We are moving to Georgia as well, closer to the sea," he said.

After three more months, Arda finally recovered from his bullet wounds in the leg and in the shoulder. It took him a few more months, however, before he could walk again on his own. But he remained weak. He had pain and limped when he stepped on his injured leg.

In the winter of 1918–1919, people were dying every day from starvation and disease. Typhus was the biggest problem. It was scary. Arda and Navart were worried for their kids. The local Armenians helped the refugees with food and shelter. From time to time, Viktor or the doctor came to see the family. Arda and Navart received some extra food and medical supplies from them. Maybe this helped them get through the cold winter.

Arda had time to think. He was tired from the seven years of war, from all the killings and destruction he had seen. It was enough.

He had nightmares while he had a fever. During one of them, in his dream he saw an old man with a long white beard telling him to get married to Navart and take her with all six kids to America. The old man told him that it was time for all of them to start a new peaceful life.

Arda remembered Ovsana had told him once of her dream when she insisted on going to Jerusalem. She had seen in her dream an old man with a long white beard.

Arda looked inside his wrist at the tattoo of Jesus Christ's head and the cross on the other hand. He had them made when they were in Jerusalem in the big Armenian church. He remembered his sister, Ovsana, and her kids, Arakssi and Hagop. They also had the same tattoos.

I wonder what they are doing now in Bulgaria. Are they well? He had abandoned them in Bulgaria. He hid from them, so he can go fight in Turkey. He was dead for them and he was embarrassed to go find them and tell them that he is alive. How he could explain this,´ when so many have died…? He thought a lot about them. He missed them. But here next to him was his new family. He had to think about them and take care of them.

Arda decided to start a new life. He asked Navart to call him Vartan, as she had called him in front of the Russian officer Viktor at the border.

"Arda is dead in East Turkey," he told Navart. "I'm your husband, Vartan, but I want us to get married again with all our kids around us in an Armenian church in America," he told her.

"Okay, Vartan," she said happily. She accepted what he said as a wish; she did not really believe that they one day could go to America.

"We will go to America some day and start a new peaceful life," Vartan said.

Navart was even happier. She had been afraid that he would start fighting again, but this time for East Armenia.

"I love you, Vartan," Navart said happily.

Vartan didn't say anything. He just pulled her close and kissed her.

Many refugees were dreaming about going to America. They already knew a lot about this country of freedom and opportunities for all emigrants.

"Armenians will be well accepted in America. It will be our country as well," Arda told Navart.

Navart smiled and did not say anything.

One day the Russian doctor came again to see Vartan. He was pleased with the improvements and asked them about their plans.

"Well, we would like to go to America and start a new life there and have more kids," Vartan said, looking at Navart.

"But I do not know how we can go there. It's just a dream I had," Vartan said, smiling at his own impossible dreams.

The doctor wished them good luck and told them that he would not be coming anymore. "There is no need for me," he said.

"Doctor, could you please take a letter I wrote to my sister in Bulgaria and mail it at the post office?" Vartan asked.

"Yes, of course. But I doubt that I can find a post office soon. Better keep it with you, and you can put it in the mail when you get to America or somewhere in Europe," he said and left the house.

At the beginning of May 1919, the Russian officer Viktor and the doctor came to Vartan in his wooden hut.

"We are going to Batumi on the Black Sea. Come with us if you still want to go to America," the officer said to Vartan.

"There is no future for Russian officers in the Bolshevik Russian Federation. Soon the Red Army will be in Armenia and Georgia. They are heading now to Azerbaijan. We have to leave. There are also Armenian officers from General Antranik's army who want to leave with us. Do you want to come?" Viktor asked Vartan.

Vartan didn't like the Bolshevik Russian Government. They had signed a treaty with Turkey leaving the Armenians in West Armenia at the mercy of the Turks and Kurds in East Turkey after the Armenians had fought side by side with them for almost four years. He thought about the Russian officers who had decided to stay with the Armenian Volunteer Army and protect the civilian population in Van and West Armenia. He had lost his country, and there were no more Armenians there.

"Yes. I will come with you, and I will take my family with me," Vartan answered.

"We have to leave right away. There is a boat in Batumi waiting for us. We will be outside," the officer said. He gave Vartan back a pistol with ammunition and a Russian officer uniform from the White Army. "This is just in case you need to protect your family."

A week later, they were standing on a Russian boat going from Batumi to Constantinople and from there to France. The boat was full with White Army Russian officers retreating from Crimea. Among them Vartan saw many Armenian officers and survivors from East Turkey. He spoke with them. He asked about General Antranik and the rest of the Armenian Volunteer Army.

An Armenian officer told him that General Antranik arrived in Zangezur with about forty thousand refugees from West Armenia. This happened right after the formation of the Republic of Armenia.

On June 4, 1918, a treaty was signed in Batumi between Turkey and Armenia. General Antranik never accepted this treaty, which left West Armenia in East Turkey. He blamed the government of New Armenia for rushing the treaty. He was disappointed and upset with them. For him, the war was not over.

His hopes were with the British Army in Iran. He tried to join his forces with the British troops in northern Iran. But the Turks pushed him back in Zangezur. The only way Turkey could reach their ally, Azerbaijan, was to go through Zangezur. General Antranik didn't allow Turkey to invade Zangezur. In the meantime, the British forces had taken Baku, Azerbaijan, on the Caspian Sea.

In October 1918, a peace treaty between the Turks and the British was signed. During the winter of 1918–1919, Antranik stayed in Zangezur. He asked the British for food provisions for the civilians during the winter, and he received some relief for them, with help as well from the Armenians living in Baku. Armenia helped them as well, with food and shelter.

General Antranik left Armenia in the spring of 1919. He had disagreements with the existing government of the new independent Armenia. He went with his army to Ecmiadzin and gave his sword to the Armenian Catholicos—the head of the Armenian Apostolic Church. This way symbolically he left his army under the Catholicos's command and his decisions. Later he went to Georgia and left from Batumi by boat to France.

Vartan and Navart held their arms around their six children while listening to the Armenian officer. Vartan was sad leaving his native Armenian land in East Turkey behind him. Only the old churches built centuries earlier were going to remind people of the Armenians once living there. But he couldn't do anything more there. He had to think now about his new family. He was now looking with hope and new worries far across the open sea.

When they were left alone, Navart pulled Vartan to herself.

"I want our child to be born as a free American. I'm pregnant, Vartan," Navart said.

Vartan put his arms around Navart and kissed her on her lips.

"We are going to have a lot of kids, Navart. Get ready for it." Vartan was now happily laughing.

"We already have six, and one more is coming. How many more do you want to have?" Navart was pretending that she was complaining, but her happy face gave her away.

May 5, 1948

Arakssi was panicking.

Her son Edwin, who had just started at the university, was very sick. He was getting weaker every day. At the beginning, he was accepted at a hospital in Plovdiv. Soon the doctors decided to move him to Sofia, where they could have the necessary medications. In Sofia, the specialists confirmed that he had pneumonia. They couldn't do anything about it.

"There is a medication against pneumonia, but it is only available in America. It is a new medication. We do not have it here," the doctor said. Then he looked around to make sure that nobody was listening and said, "Listen, we are living in a communist Bulgaria, and we cannot ask Americans to send us this medication. We will be accused of having connections with the imperialists."

He looked around again and continued, "You Armenians should have some relatives there, or you can ask through your Armenian church for help from the American Red Cross. You have to ask for streptomycin," he said.

Arakssi was looking and listening with hope in her eyes.

"But it is going to take a lot of time. How much time do we have?" she asked the doctor.

"I do not know exactly. He is young, and his body is strong. Maybe we have a month; at the max, forty-five days," the doctor said.

"Ask for ten doses of streptomycin, enough to cure ten people. This way, I will convince the communist management of the hospital to accept the medication and to preserve one dose for your son," he added.

Back in the train on her way home, Arakssi was crying; her son Santo and her daughter, Vera, tried to calm her down and give her hope.

"I will speak with the Armenian priest tomorrow," Santo promised her.

"I will write a letter to the American Red Cross in Armenian. Somebody there will translate it into English," Vera told her mother. She was only fourteen years old, but she was smart—always the first in her school.

"Mom, I'm very good at writing. You know my teacher is always giving me the best grades," she continued.

Arakssi was sobbing.

"It will take time. Everything is so slow. A letter to America will take at least three weeks. By the time somebody decides what to do with it, that will take a few more days. Then they have to send the medications to Sofia as a parcel. That will take three more weeks. It has to go through customs, which will take one more week. And this entire thing depends on if the Red Cross agrees to help us and the communist authorities allow us to have the medication for my son." She started crying again.

"Mom, they have invented a telegraph. We will ask the priest to send a telegram to an Armenian church in America," Santo said to calm her down.

"We have to convince the communist authorities. Sending a telegram outside Bulgaria will be possible only with special permission," Santo continued.

"Maybe the Armenian priest can help with this also?" Arakssi asked, getting some new hope.

"Okay, Mom, tomorrow we will go together to the priest with a letter already written," Santo said, now looking at Vera.

"What? That's too fast. I'm not ready with the letter," Vera said in panic.

"So, stop talking and start writing your letter. We have enough time on the train. Let's see how good you are," Santo said.

They stopped talking. Vera took out a pen and a notebook from her bag and put them on her lap. She quickly wrote down what she was feeling and what thoughts came to her. She was overexcited, and when she finished, she had written four pages. She handed them to Santo.

Santo looked at her and said, "Now, write it again, but in one page only!"

She looked at him and then at her mother with an upset face. "Mom, please take the letter I have ready. I cannot write about the life of my dying brother and ask for compassion in one page," she said emotionally.

Arakssi turned to Vera and said, "Vera, please write it again, but maximum in two pages. Nobody will have the patience to read a longer letter asking for help."

Arakssi closed her eyes, trying to calm down. She thought about her mother Ovsana. She missed her so much. She would have told her what to do. She would have hugged her and given her hope. She would have found a solution. She always did for them. Ovsana passed away in 1941 when she was just forty-nine years old. At least she was able to see her grandchildren, Santo, Edwin, and Vera.

Arakssi remembered her last conversation with her mother:

"I will miss my grandchildren." Ovsana's eyes filled with tears.

"I will always be around you when you need me. Do not be afraid. You are strong. You will be able to take care of your family!" she told Arakssi, and she squeezed her hand one last time.

"Mom, I need you ..." she whispered.

Later that same night at home, she couldn't sleep. Her husband, Agop, was already asleep next to her. In the other room was Santo. And in the other room, Vera was sleeping.

Arakssi was emotionally exhausted. Finally when she was very tired, she fell asleep for maybe ten minutes. She woke up scared. In her dream, she had seen her mom. Ovsana was seated next to the mailbox in her house, and she was reading a letter. Then she picked up a second letter, and she put it down next to the first one. She carefully wrapped a blue ribbon around the two letters.

Then Arakssi really woke up. It was like waking up from a double dream. Was she really asleep, or was her tired brain playing games with her?

She was shaking. It had been so real in her dream. She saw her mother reading those two letters and then putting them to one side, as if she wanted Arakssi to read them as well. She had seen this box before. Ovsana kept it locked in her room in her house. Now her brother, Hagop, was living there alone.

Hagop was much better than when he was a boy. But still he was not very good. He was able to work, but not for too long. Every place he started working became difficult for him, and after about six months, he had to leave and look for a new job. He came to Arakssi's house every week to see her and her husband, Agop, and her kids. She gave him warm food, and sometimes she washed his shirt as well. Every two weeks she went to his house with Vera, and together they cleaned the house, put everything in order, and washed his clothes. It was like having one older child. He was already thirty-six years old.

About seven years ago, soon after Ovsana passed away, he started bringing women to his mother's home. He was a handsome man, and women chased after him. Usually they stayed with him for a few days, a week or two, and then they ran away. He missed them for a while, but soon he forgot them.

One of these girls got pregnant, but she also didn't stay long. She gave birth to a beautiful and completely normal boy. She named his son Martin. She remained close to Arakssi's family, and they helped her take care of Hagop's son. When he was six years old, his mother would bring him to Arakssi's home and sometimes to the shop. He studied, played, and grew as all normal boys. He loved coming to their home and seeing Aunty Arakssi and Uncle Agop. His cousins—Santo, Vera, and Edwin—were much bigger than he was, and usually they were not at home when he came over.

Arakssi got up early in the morning. She prepared breakfast for everybody, and before the house woke up, she went over to her mother's house.

She had a key for the house, and she entered. Hagop was still sleeping in his room, and she left him a piece of the cake she had prepared for breakfast. Then she entered her mother's room. She kept it locked all the time, and she had the only key. She didn't want anybody touching her mom's clothes and her personal belongings.

The room was the same as it had been seven years earlier. Her brother liked looking in when Arakssi was there, and he always said, with a smile on his handsome face, "Where is Mom? Is she coming soon?"

"Do not touch anything if you want her to come back!" Arakssi would say, and he never entered the room or touched anything.

Arakssi went inside, leaving the door open, and turned on the light. She went straight to the night table next to her mother's bed, and she took out her letter box.

There were many letters from her friends, but she couldn't find the two letters wrapped with a blue ribbon.

She left the letters in the box, and she started looking around for the two letters she saw in her dream.

"Yes, this was just the dream of a desperate mother looking for miracles," she said aloud.

"Mom, is that you?" she heard Hagop calling from his room.

"Hagop, I am your sister, Arakssi," she said. "Put on your clothes! Go wash yourself and go to the kitchen. I have made breakfast for you. I will come in a few minutes," she called out from her mother's room.

In a few minutes, Hagop came to the door of his mother's room.

"Mom was here last night," he said.

Arakssi was not paying attention to him. It was not the first time she had heard the same thing. She was opening the drawers of the night table and checking them carefully.

"Are you looking for this?" Hagop asked, holding in his hand a small package wrapped with a blue ribbon.

"Where did you find them?" Arakssi asked, surprised.

"I told you, Mom was here. She was reading these letters, and she left them for you," Hagop said and showed her the letters.

Arakssi was now standing in the middle of the room with a hand over her mouth. She was now more scared than when she woke up from the dream seeing her mother leaving her two letters wrapped in a blue ribbon.

"Hagop, how did you enter the room? I keep it locked. I told you not to go inside." Arakssi was now upset with her brother, or maybe she was just scared and talking loudly.

"I just wanted to help your son Edwin. He is not going to die, is he?" Hagop was scared, and he took his sister's hand.

"I love my little nephew Ed. I'm not going to let him die. Mom told us about these letters when she was dying. She told us if we needed help to write letters to Uncle Metho and Uncle Arda …" Hagop was talking fast and squeezing his sister's arm.

"Uncle Arda is dead," Arakssi said.

"No, he is not. My mom told me that she knows he is alive and he is in America." Hagop was now crying.

"Mom told me he is alive and he will help us if we need help," he kept repeating.

"Okay, Hagop. I believe you. Give these letters to me and let me read them." Arakssi started talking with a calming voice, as if she were talking to a small child.

"Go wash your face and go to the kitchen. I will come with you and make you tea. Do you want tea?" she asked him.

"Yes, I do. But please write letters to Uncle Metho and Uncle Arda. They will come here and help my nephew Ed," Hagop repeated again, and then he went to the kitchen.

She walked with Hagop to the kitchen, taking the letters with her. She sat down at the table.

The first letter was from Methody Terziev. It was dated 1940. It was thick.

She remembered Uncle Metho. She had good memories of him.

When she opened it, she found ten letters put together in the same envelope. There were letters from 1925 till 1940. They were written in the old Turkish – Arabic script. Thank God she knew reading and writing in this language. Her mother had insisted her to learn it when she was going to the Armenian school and there were as well classes in Turkish. Armenians hoped one day they could go back to their homes…Just to visit and see where they were born, where their ancestors had been borne few thousand years ago...

She read the first letter quickly. Methody was talking about himself. He was writing about his son and what he was doing. He told her how much he was hurt when he learned that his wife already had married again, thinking that he was dead. She had written many letters to their village in Turkey, but the letters kept coming back. The village did not exist anymore.

Metho asked Ovsana to come to America, and they could live there together with her son and his son as well. His wife already had two more kids with her new husband.

Arakssi was surprised. She didn't know if her mother had answered his first letter, so she kept reading the letters, one after another.

Metho was saying that he loved her and he knew that she could not leave her family and her grandchildren. He told her that he could not leave his son. His son loved his father and his mother very much, and Metho loved him as well and wanted to give him full support and help him get a good education. He was working as a carpenter.

In one of his letters, Metho told her that he bought a new house, and now he lived with his son in their new home. He was still hoping that she could come to live with him in Chicago one day. He asked her to let him know if she needed anything. He would love to help her or her family.

She saw the address of his new home written on his letter.

Oh, Mom, you never asked Uncle Metho for anything, but you showed me his letters. I will ask him to save my son. Arakssi felt new hope in her heart.

She took the letter and put it in her pocket. Then she put all of the rest in the envelope and put it back in the box. Then she picked up the second envelope.

It was dated 1920, and it was written in Armenian by a woman named Navart. The letter came from Boston, United States of America.

The letter talked about her uncle Ardashes and his last days in East Turkey.

It told his sister, Ovsana, about the last three weeks of his life. Navart went into detail how he saved her life and the lives of her two children. It was a long letter telling her the stories that Ardashes had told her during the long nights in the shelters—stories about his fights for freedom, as well as his desire for peace and a new life full of love and happiness.

She told Ovsana that Ardashes had told her about his sister and her two kids and asked her if something happened to him to write a letter to the Armenian church in Shumen, Bulgaria, and ask the priest to give the letter to Ovsana Kaladian.

"He knew that you were alive in Bulgaria, and he asked me to contact you and give you my new address once we got out of Turkey and offer you help anytime you needed it."

She wrote how on the last day before crossing the border, he had saved the lives of four more Armenian kids and he wanted to adopt them as well as her children.

"Arda offered to become my husband and father to all the kids. I accepted, and in front of God, we are married."

Then she wrote that she had immigrated to America and was now in Boston. She wrote down her address and asked Ovsana to keep in touch.

At the end, she said that she had given birth in America to a son. She called him Arda after the name of his father, Ardashes.

"P.S. Arda is alive for me and my family ..." she wrote at the very bottom of her letter after finishing it—as if she wanted to tell Ovsana something more.

There was one more letter from Navart, dated 1925. She was giving her new address in Boston, where she bought a house and moved with her family. She was asking Ovsana to keep in touch and to right her back.

Arakssi immediately started writing her own letters.

She wrote one letter to Methody, with an address in Chicago, USA, and one to Navart, with an address in Boston, USA.

It was a short letter—one page—just saying who she was and explaining why she was asking for their help.

"Please hurry up. My son Edwin is sick with pneumonia. He is in the general hospital in Sofia, and the doctor is asking for ten doses of streptomycin to be able to cure ten people. He has given Edwin a maximum of forty-five days to be saved. Please contact the American Red Cross to receive permission from the communist authorities in Bulgaria to accept the help.

"I pray to God to save my son.

"With hope and love,

"Arakssi, daughter of Ovsana Kaladian."

She wrote the date, sealed the letters, and addressed the envelopes, including her return address.

Then she went to the post office and asked for the fastest way to send these two letters to America. She explained to the officer working there why she was rushing, and she gave him the letters with shaking hands.

Please, God, save my son, she prayed.

It was already noon when she got home. She didn't say anything. Santo and Vera were waiting for her. Vera was ready with her letter, and Santo was inpatient to go and speak with the Armenian priest.

"Where were you?" Agop asked her. "Santo and Vera are waiting for you. Hurry up. Go with them to see the priest," Agop said with a shaking voice.

"Come with us, Agop," she said to her husband.

"Okay. I'm coming. Give me a few minutes to get dressed," he answered and rushed to the bathroom to shave his face.

June 11, 1948

It was Edwin's birthday. He was turning eighteen years old.

Agop, Arakssi, Santo, and Vera were in Sofia and wanted to visit Ed and wish him quick recovery, good health, and a long and happy life.

Arakssi and Santo came to Sofia every other day and went back to Plovdiv in the afternoon.

There was no news from the American Red Cross, and they were all getting more and more worried. Ed was coughing and breathing heavily. He had a high fever. His face had turned pale. He was weak and didn't have any appetite. But every time he saw his family, he smiled at them.

"*Mi goular Mama. Yes lav bedi ulam.* Do not cry, Mom. I will get better," Edwin would say and smile at them.

Agop, Arakssi, Santo, and Vera entered the hospital with mixed feelings. They were afraid for Edwin, and they were hoping for a miracle. It was the thirty-seventh day since he was accepted in the hospital. It was the thirty-fifth day since they had sent a letter to the

Armenian church in California. The Armenian priest from Plovdiv had personal connections with the priest of the Armenian church in Glendale, California. He had sent his letter together with Vera's letter asking for help to save the life of a young Armenian man. Vera's letter was so emotional that it would make anyone cry. In his letter the priest prayed to God to save Edwin's life, and at the end, he wrote that Edwin's uncle, Ardashes Hadjiahparian, had saved the lives of many Armenians in East Turkey in 1918 as a volunteer under the command of General Antranik. He closed with, "God, please help us now save the life of his nephew Edwin."

The doctor met them in the corridor, smiling happily.

"They arrived yesterday—an Armenian priest from America and two American representatives of the American Red Cross. One of them speaks Bulgarian. The other two are of Armenian origin," the doctor said excitedly.

"We already gave him two injections, and Edwin is feeling much better today. It is a miracle. I cannot believe this is really happening. He is recovering so quickly," he said while he led them to Edwin's room.

Arakssi and Agop were crying loudly from happiness. Vera and Santo were smiling, and Santo kissed his sister on her cheek.

"Bravo, Vera, you saved your brother," Santo said.

"No, we all did it, as well as these men who came here all the way from America," Vera said.

They all entered the room after the doctor. Edwin was sitting up in the bed and eating his lunch hungrily. Arakssi was the first to hug him and wish him a happy birthday. They all did. They were all talking now at the same time and laughing. Edwin took the chocolate bar Santo had bought for him.

"*Manch, inch pess ess?* Boy, how are you doing?" Santo asked his brother, the same way he used to ask him when Ed was three years old. This tradition had remained between them, and they often called each other *manch*—boy.

"*Manch, tun inch pess ess?* Boy, how are you?" Ed asked Santo in return, smiling.

"Honestly, I could not be happier," Santo said, laughing.

"*Haide!* Come on! Get better and come home. I'm getting tired of coming to Sofia every other day," Santo said, pretending that he was complaining.

Arakssi and Agop were listening to their kids talking and joking.

The doctor came back again in about an hour.

"The Armenian priest and the two representatives of the American Red Cross are in my office. They came to say good-bye to Edwin and his family; they are going back to the airport," the doctor said. "They have brought enough streptomycin to save the lives of at least thirty people. Our hospital administration is very thankful to them."

"Can I speak first with them alone?" Arakssi asked. "I need just ten minutes. I want to thank them ... please give me some privacy," Arakssi continued, seeing that the doctor's reaction at first was negative.

"I might lose my job for that, if somebody reports me to the administration ... Okay, come with me to my office," he said, not very enthusiastically.

Arakssi put on a white nurse's coat. She entered the room alone and closed the door after herself.

They were seated in front of the doctor's desk. The priest was in black clothes with a black pelerine and a black hood on his head, a long chain and a silver cross hanging around his neck. The other two men were dressed in suits with ties; they were in their late fifties or early sixties, with already-gray hair.

She took off her white coat and introduced herself. "I'm Arakssi, Edwin's mother," she said while she looked in the eyes of the three men.

They all stood up, and before anybody else said anything, Arakssi came close to the priest, took his hand, and kissed it.

"Thank you for your help, father. You saved the life of my boy," she said, now sobbing, but this time with happiness.

"You have to thank God. He has helped you," the priest said simply.

Then Arakssi turned to the taller man. He held a cane in his left hand. His blue eyes looked at her with a smile.

"Uncle Metho, is that you?" Arakssi asked.

"Yes. It is me, and you look just like your mother, Ovsana," he said, his eyes now full of tears.

"Thank you for saving my son. I knew you would come." She hugged him as she used to do when she was young.

The third man was looking at her with burning black eyes under his big gray eyebrows. His mustache was still black, but his beard was white and his hair gray.

"Arakssi, tun ess? Is that you?" he asked in Armenian and came close to her.

"Uncle Arda, you are alive?" she asked, surprised. "My brother Hagop kept on telling me that you were alive. I cannot believe it," she said and hugged him. "Why didn't you tell us that you were alive? My mom could have been so happy," she said.

Arda looked down uncomfortably.

"Honestly, when I remained alive after leaving East Turkey and our land, I felt guilty for remaining alive. I was injured and weak for many months, and I couldn't do anything more for West Armenia. My country was destroyed. Armenians from my land were either exterminated or dispersed all over the world. I started a new peaceful life with my wife, Navart, and our nine kids in Boston in the United States. Time has passed, and for years I was not comfortable saying who I am. Then it was late to tell my sister that I was alive." He was still looking down at his feet.

"Arda, my friend, you are alive," Metho said in Turkish. He came close to Arda, and then he too hugged him. "I was told by a common Armenian friend, Aram, that you died defending a high mountain passage, saving the lives of many Armenians who were fleeing Van," Metho said.

"No, I was able to escape, and later I found Navart with her two small kids wandering in the bush, and then later I was able to take back from the Kurds four more Armenian kids. We were all able to come out of Turkey. A Russian officer helped us to stay for a year in Georgia, and then from Batumi we went to America. I marred Navart and adopted all six kids. Since then, I had three more kids with Navart. We started a new life in Boston, where there is a big Armenian community," Arda said, also in Turkish.

"My new name is Vartan. I want it to stay this way," he added, looking at Arakssi.

"Yes, I have to ask you not to reveal your identity to my family or to the local communist authorities. You do not know what it is to live in a communist country. My kids will have no future if they find out that we are relatives or friends. We will be tagged as dangerous for the Bulgarian socialist society and potential enemies for spreading capitalist propaganda," Arakssi explained quickly in Turkish.

"How come the three of you came together?" she asked, again in Turkish so everybody would be able to understand at the same time.

The priest started talking in Turkish as well. "When I contacted the American Red Cross agent responsible for Eastern Europe, he told me that two more people separately and without knowing about each other had requested the same thing: to go to Sofia and help an Armenian boy, Edwin Azadian. They both offered to pay for all the expenses. They each asked the American Red Cross to negotiate the donation of ten doses of streptomycin on behalf of the Armenian church in the United States, with the condition that one full dose, enough to completely recover a sick man from pneumonia, be given to Edwin." The priest continued to explain how the Red Cross ended up organizing the donation of enough streptomycin to heal at least thirty people from pneumonia.

Somebody knocked on the door, and then without waiting, opened the door. It was the doctor.

"Please, Arakssi, you have to leave now. Please put on the white coat and go to your son's room. We will come along in a few minutes so our guests can see Edwin and his family and after that go right to the airport. A special car from hospital security is waiting downstairs for them," he told her in Bulgarian.

Arakssi left, while Metho translated into English what the doctor said.

In ten minutes, the Armenian priest and the two representatives of the American Red Cross came into the room, accompanied by the doctor and a security man from the hospital who had just arrived.

Arakssi, Agop, Vera, and Santo kissed the priest's hand and thanked him in Armenian for the generous donation and for saving Edwin's life. They shook the hands of the two representatives of the American Red Cross and also thanked them for coming all the way to Sofia and helping their son and brother to recover.

The priest gave them all his blessing, and shortly after that they left the room and the hospital, heading directly to the airport.

Arakssi was crying while the people from the Red Cross looked down at their feet as they walked out.

"Such serious people! They never smiled or said a word to us. They didn't even notice us," Vera said, upset.

Arakssi started crying louder, and she hugged her daughter.

November 1956

Santo was in a small room in the basement of the local Communist Police Department for the second day. He didn't even know why they had arrested him. He had done nothing against the law.

"Write down what you have done!" the inspector told him, giving him an empty notebook and a pencil.

They had forgotten him in this small room with no heating and no bed. There was only a table and two chairs and a lamp hanging from the ceiling on a long cord. In the corner there was a toilet pot made of baked clay.

He had no food and no water. An empty cup still sat on the table. The inspector gave it to him full of water before leaving him alone.

"It will be much better for you if you tell us voluntarily what you have done against your communist country," the inspector said with a chilly coldness in his voice.

These were difficult years for intellectuals and entrepreneurs in Bulgaria. Between 1952 and 1956, many people disappeared into special camps built for the political enemies of the communist regime. The worst of all was Belene. Saying anything against the communists was enough cause to be arrested. If they believed that you could potentially be dangerous to the regime, they would send you to these camps.

Santo forced himself to think of something pleasant. His brother, Edwin, got married. His sister married as well. Last year, Santo had a son, Eric, in June 1955. A few months after that, Edwin had a daughter, Alexa, and his sister gave birth also to a daughter, Victoria. His wife, Nelly, stayed at home, looking after Lisa and Eric. She also helped Arakssi with the housework and was learning Armenian from her and Agop. Santo smiled when he remembered how well Nelly was now speaking Armenian. She had the same accent as his father, Agop.

Santo started thinking again about his work at the shop. Life was getting difficult because his father often was sick in the last seven years and was not able to work in his shop. Santo had to work twice as much to be able to deliver on time and provide for his family. His wife, Nelly, helped him from time to time when she was not busy with the kids. His father had gotten special permission from the communists to keep his shop because he had presented them documents that he was sick. Nobody except his family could work in it. Any other private ownership of a shop or factory was forbidden and confiscated by the government.

Santo did not bang on the door or shout for help, as he had heard people doing in the other rooms in the basement. He knew the authorities ignored him on purpose, and not because they had forgotten him. This was part of the torture. This was part of the communist way to keep people scared and in complete control. Who would have the guts to say we were not happy to live under communist rule? In the schools, the kids were told how lucky they were to be born in our sunny socialist Bulgaria. However, nobody was allowed to go out and visit friends or relatives living in the dying capitalist world. The truth was that the communist authorities were afraid people would find out how poor we actually are in Bulgaria.

He had lost all sense of time when finally his door was opened and the same inspector came in. The inspector looked at the empty notebook and just told Santo to come upstairs with him.

Before entering his office, the inspector told him to go to the toilet room and refresh himself.

Once he entered the office, the inspector offered him the chair in front of his desk. On the other side of the desk was seated a man in a suit and tie.

"Santo, we checked you out. You are clean. However, your permission to work in the shop is taken away. You have to sign here that you are donating your shop to the people of Bulgaria, and state on this document that you want to start working at the shoe factory as a shoe designer," the inspector said.

"We heard very good reports about your ability to design new models. This will be used for the interest of our country," the man in the suit said.

"May I ask you why you have arrested me?" Santo asked.

The inspector laughed. "We have good citizens who are constantly reporting to us what everybody does. We were told that you bought chocolates every day. That was suspicious. We decided to check if you were properly reporting all your expenses and incomes."

"You are lucky that you wrote everything down in your notebook in the shop day by day—everything you bought and everything you sold," the suited man told him.

"Otherwise, you would be going to Belene," he said, seeming almost unhappy that this was not the case.

"My son, Eric, was sick, and the only thing he could eat was chocolate," Santo said, not believing his ears. He was arrested because he loved his son and had bought him chocolates every day. That was disgusting.

Grandma, how could you come to this country instead of going to Western Europe or America? Santo was thinking, but he did not show any emotions.

I hope my kids will be able to go to America one day and live there far from the communists. The whole country is a prison, Santo wanted to cry aloud, but instead he just smiled.

"Yes, here in the Communist Police Department, we know everything," the inspector proudly said.

Santo didn't say anything. He signed the document, and he was told to go to work the next day at the shoe factory. All the belongings in the shop, including his machines and tools, were confiscated by the government. They had taken his key when they arrested him. He couldn't even go and take his personal belongings from the shop, and he didn't ask for them.

"You are a free man, Santo. You are lucky to live in a socialist country, Bulgaria, where everybody is equal and has the right and obligation to work. By the way, your wife has to go to work in the same factory as soon as your son gets better," the inspector told him. Then the inspector shook his hand good-bye, as if the inspector were his friend or a business partner.

When Santo entered his house, his wife, Nelly, and his mother, Arakssi, started crying and hugged him with relief. Edwin and Agop gathered around him and were looking at him to see if he were all right.

"I'm okay. Everything is okay. It was a mistake. The only thing is that the government took our shop, along with everything inside. Tomorrow I'm starting to work in the shoe factory," Santo said. He went to wash his face and hands with soap. "I'm hungry and thirsty, and I feel dirty," he said simply.

Nelly prepared a plate with food and filled a glass with water, while Arakssi started warming water on the oven in the kitchen so he could take a bath. Edwin was standing next to him and watching him.

"Manch, you are very upset. What happened?" Edwin asked.

"Nothing, nothing unexpected happened," Santo said. "Let's leave this conversation for another time. I'm really tired, and I want to see my kids," Santo said now, turning to Nelly.

"How is Eric doing? How is Lisa? Where are they?" he asked.

"They are doing well. They are upstairs in our room sleeping," Nelly answered.

"I'm glad you are back home, Santo," Edwin said, tapping him on the shoulder.

"Yes, I know. How are Alexa and Nadia doing?" he asked.

"They are fine. Nadia is trying to put Alexa to sleep. She was crying, but she is fine. Vera, Manuk, and Victoria are also good. They were here an hour ago, and they left before dinner," Edwin said.

"How are we going to live without our shop?" Agop asked suddenly, with tears in his eyes. "I opened this shop in 1923 before getting married to your mother. We had it for thirty-three years, and we survived because of it. It supported you all. Santo and I worked in it, and we were able to provide for all of you while you were growing up. Now how are we going to survive?"

Agop was crying. "It was my life … I do not feel good … Arakssi, please call a doctor!" He was sobbing.

"You do not need a doctor. Take these pills. They will calm you down in ten minutes," Arakssi said, giving him two pills.

"What are these pills?" Santo asked Edwin in a low voice.

"Oh, they are just valerian, but we told him that they are special and Vera found them through her connections especially for him. He calls them Vera's pills. And they really are the best thing he has taken so far," Edwin said, smiling.

Santo went to his father and told him, "Dad, do not worry. We will be fine. I'm going to work in the shoe factory as a shoe designer and process manager. I'm starting tomorrow. Nelly will start working soon as well. I will manage to bring some work for you to do at home, so you can work whenever you feel good. I will finish your work when I come home from the factory. This way we will have three people working. It will be enough to pay for the mortgage and for food and clothes and heating during the winter."

Santo was talking to his father calmly and with confidence. It looked like it was working. His father started to calm down and was no longer calling for a doctor.

"I'm also working now, and I will not let you down," Edwin said with a firm voice, standing on the other side of his father.

Agop was now even smiling. "Thank God we have such good kids, Arakssi," Agop said to his wife.

"Do not worry, Arakssi!" Agop was now trying to give courage to his wife. "We will manage, I'm sure. It's just that I feel so sad. Why did they have to take our small shop?" He was still upset while talking to his wife.

"We don't have a choice, Dad. It is a miracle they let us keep it for so long. Everybody else lost their shops and factories, and it's good they did not send me to Belene," Santo said.

"One thing, for sure: I will not let my kids become communists," Santo said and went upstairs to join his wife and kids in their room.

September 2013

Eric was working on the book in his office. He was coming to the end of his stories about his father and mother. Something was bothering him. Something was missing, and he didn't know what it was. Slowly he came to realize that he didn't have many different memories about them. It was as if they were invisible ...

He thought about his father and his mother. How did they live during these years when communism was so strong and brutal in Bulgaria? They were turned into prisoners together with millions of other people who did not accept becoming communists. They were slowly turned into shadows of people, with no dreams or hope. They were turned into people who preferred not to be in the spotlight, to be invisible. They had very little personal time. The only pleasures left were to quickly enjoy the smiles of their children, family love, a well-finished job at work, the beauty of nature, music, art, books about the outside world, achievements in sports, and knowledge gained in schools and the university.

Slowly many people started losing even these last signs of human dignity. People were forced to be equal in the lack of ambition. Equal in the guaranteed bare minimum for food on the table, medical help, housing, work that didn't pay you much no matter how hard you pushed yourself. Equal in the maximum you could have. Equal in your unimportance in the society where you lived.

Then why push yourself? What happens with creativity if the only thing you get is a tap on your shoulder and respect from your boss? Eric thought.

How can you live without dreams and hopes for a better life?

How can you live without the freedom to travel the world?

How can you live without freedom of speech?

How can you live without the freedom to pray to your God and have hope?

How can you live all the time in fear that if you say or if you do something wrong, you will be arrested?

Eric tried to remember more about his parents.

Why do I not remember much about my parents? Were they not interesting people, or I was a bad son who did not care what they were doing?

Eric remembered his father, Santo, and his mother, Nelly, getting up early in the mornings at 4:30 a.m. They turned on the radio and started to talk in low voices so as not to wake him up. They talked about the work. In fifteen minutes, his mother was pushing him to get up with them.

"Eric, if you want to become successful one day, get up now. Do your gymnastics and start learning your lessons so you can be the best in school," Nelly said to Eric when he was a small boy.

"Then what am I going to do when I become the best in school?" Eric asked.

"Then you will be smart enough to decide what you will do so you can have a better life than we have now," she said and kissed him on the cheek.

They left at 5:30 a.m. to go to work, while Eric studied the new lessons that the teacher was going to give them that day. His mother always told him that he had to be prepared in advance, and then he would do better than everybody else.

He hid this small secret, which helped him most of the time to be slightly ahead of the majority.

His parents came home about three thirty. They slept for about an hour, and at 5:00 p.m., they started working again.

Eric remembered the smell of acetone from the glue they used on the shoe parts. He felt dizzy from it when he stayed with them in the small room. He liked joining them and doing some work, but the smell of acetone made him vomit even though the windows were open. His mother always sent him out to finish his homework and study more. Santo and Nelly were finishing the work his grandfather Agop couldn't complete during the day, and about seven thirty, they were ready for supper. The next day, everything repeated again from the beginning.

One day his father told him that he had to get registered in sports. He was eleven years old when he went with his father to a special building for training kids in different sports after school.

"You need to learn how to protect yourself," his father said and suggested boxing or wrestling.

"I don't want his nose to be broken," his mother said.

So Eric ended up registering in wrestling and in gymnastics.

Eric trained every afternoon for three hours in the sports building, which was not far from their home.

He liked both the wrestling and the gymnastics, where he learned how to jump over obstacles and turn in the air before landing again on his legs; how to play on the horse, on the two parallel bars, and on the hanging circle handles; and many other things. He was pretty good in both sports, and the trainer was encouraging him to continue.

When he became fourteen years old, he had to choose to go to a sports school or to a regular high school.

His mother got involved and said, "Enough with the sports. Let him now study literature, geography, history, and science, and then go to the university."

When he was in high school, sometimes during lunch Eric went to see his parents at the factory, which was just across the street. He found out that Santo had become the manager of the product-development department and his mother, Nelly, was the floor manager of about sixty women working on a conveyer. The women teased him so he didn't feel comfortable staying there, but he liked joining his father. There were about fifteen people working in his department, and there the new models of shoes were coming alive.

Santo showed him around to his colleagues and then explained to him the process of making the shoes and what every person in his department was doing. Then he took Eric through the factory and explained how everything worked from the beginning to the end. Eric liked the smell of the shoes and the leather. He was amazed by the machines and how they did different things to the leather. His father explaining about how the work was organized and how important it was that everybody in the line of production be well-prepared for the new shoe models and what materials and machines could be used so the quality would be good and the process efficient.

His mother was the manager on the floor. She told him her secret to being a good manager in production: "Be knowledgeable and hands-on. Manage people with strong hands covered in velour gloves and smile," she told him in a low voice so nobody could hear.

She was always smiling and in a good mood, but he noticed that the women were afraid of her and they listened to her orders.

When Eric was seventeen, it was time to go to the army for two years to do his military service. He remembered his father, Santo, going to the railway station with him early in the morning. There were hundreds of young men like him. Most of them were together with their entire families. Mothers and fathers were crying and continually giving the boys advice. Eric and Santo stood there silently watching, as if they were just observers. Finally an officer came out and asked all the young men to get on the train and the parents to calm down.

"We will take good care of your kids. When they come back, they will be men. Don't worry! Nothing bad will happen to them," the officer shouted loudly.

Eric turned to his father and shook his hand.

"Listen to the officers and do what they tell you. Do not volunteer, but if they give you an order, do it!" Santo said and slapped him on the back.

"Okay. Dad, don't worry about me. I will be fine," Eric said and jumped on the train.

Eric wanted to remember more about his father and mother, but the only way he could do that was to continue the thin string of his memories as they came.

It bothered him that his father told him so little when he entered the army, but with time, he realized that his father gave him the best advice: "Listen to the officers and do what they tell you."

The first three months were tough—even though everybody knew that this was a tradition in the army.

The old soldiers tried to make the newcomers cry, tried to break them. The officers closed their eyes as if this were part of the training and had nothing to do with them.

Early in the morning at five o'clock, the sergeant came into the room, turned the lights on, and shouting for everybody to be up, dressed, and out of the building in ten seconds.

This was impossible, but it didn't matter. It was part of the training to ask for shockingly impossible things. But he was surprised to see that the four old soldiers who were chosen to help the sergeant were able to get ready first. They were screaming now at the top of their lungs to make the newcomers move faster. It just added pressure to the whole thing. When they finally got out, dressed in pantaloons, boots, and T-shirts, they were lined up in front of the sergeant.

"Next time you have to get out faster. It took you two minutes. Now we are going to do that again. Go back to your room. Take off your clothes and go to bed. Now go!" the sergeant shouted loudly.

They repeated it a few times, and every time the old soldiers were first. Eric finally noticed they were not taking off their trousers when they went to bed.

The next morning, Eric woke up at 4:30 a.m. He carefully got out of bed and put on his trousers; then he went to bed again. When the sergeant came and ordered them out, Eric was among the first in line in front of the building.

The old soldiers still asked the newcomers to do all kinds of stupid and absurd things just for the fun of it. They would ask them to do push-ups till they got tired, to clean the floor with toothbrushes, to jump on one leg till they fell down, to dress in two seconds—and when you couldn't do it, you had to repeat it again and again.

One day a few high-ranking officers came along with their officer and announced that they would interrogate all the young soldiers one by one and hear if they had any complaints. Somebody had sent them a letter with information about psychological abuse of the young soldiers beyond the normal training. They had come to check if this were true. When Eric came in the room in front of the officers, they asked him if he had any complaints.

"No, sir, I have no complaints," Eric answered.

Then an older officer asked him, "Soldier, do you want to ask for something?"

Eric thought about that for a moment and then said, "Yes, sir."

"What is it, private?" the officer asked him.

"I would like to have a few minutes' time to wash my hands before we go to eat, sir," Eric said.

The next day the officers were gone, and nothing had really changed. When it was time to go to the cafeteria to eat, though, his sergeant waited for them to wash their hands.

The sergeant asked Eric before they entered the dining room, "Private Azadian, did you have time to wash your hands?" His face was serious, but his eyes were smiling. He was not upset with Eric.

Eric was not a tall soldier. When they lined up, he stood somewhere in the shorter half of the soldiers. One day after they exercised all day, they went in the barracks before going to bed. One of the old soldiers came to Eric and started pushing him. He was at least a full head taller than Eric. Eric stood still and waited for the higher-in-rank soldier to stop pushing him around. But he didn't.

Eric's hands started to shake. Only his closest friend knew that this was not from fear, but because of the effort he was making to keep himself calm.

"Look at this little boy. He is going to cry for his mom now," the old soldier said, laughing loudly. His face was still smiling when suddenly he found himself on the ground on his back.

The room became silent. All the soldiers were shocked.

Eric took a few steps to the soldier and extended his hand to help him up. But the soldier was upset, and now he shouted that he would kick Eric. His intentions were clear, and Eric stepped back to get ready for his attacker. Now his hands were not shaking anymore. He had made a decision to fight back. But it was not necessary.

A friend of his from high school came out and said to the old soldier, "Don't be silly. You have no chance fighting him. He was a champion in wrestling at high school."

Eric turned his back to the old soldier and started preparing his bed, totally ignoring him. He took off his clothes, put them in order on the small night table, and jumped in the bed.

Time passed quickly. Eric came back from the army in two years, and he went to the university. After graduating, he married Renee. She had graduated from the same university. Then they started working. Then the kids came. First was Nevena, and then a few years later, Maya. Eric and Renee were happy, as all young people in love are.

Ten years later, Eric had become a manager of a biotech engineering team with about fifteen people. One day he met the marketing director of the corporation he was working at. He remembered him. He used to be the marketing director of the shoe factory when his father worked there. Santo had just retired a year ago. The marketing director was happy to find out that he was Santo's son. He told Eric about how his father had saved the factory from closing.

"The regional Communist Party committee that was responsible for the economic development of Plovdiv raised the question of the future of the shoe factory. Other shoe factories were more successful. We had three months to come up with new, better models and lower prices so we could have new contracts for the next year.

"Your father, who was at that time a simple designer, came to me with an incredible collection of shoes, and we got the most government contracts for the next year. The same year, we made him manager of the product-development department," the director told him.

"He could have achieved much more if he was a communist member," the marketing director told Eric. Then he asked Eric, "Why don't you become a communist? You should consider joining the Communist Party if you want to grow in the corporation," he said, smiling at him in a friendly way.

"I'm still too young for this and too busy with my work," Eric answered, and he changed the subject.

In 1989, after the fall of the Berlin Wall, which symbolically represented the collapse of communism in the Eastern Block and the Soviet Union, the communist regime in Bulgaria fell. In the winter of 1990, there were demonstrations of a million people on the streets of Sofia. The Bulgarian legislature was forced to delete from the constitution the "leading role" of the Communist Party. Soon after that, in the spring of 1990, the Communist Party renamed itself the Bulgarian Socialist Party (BSP). They abandoned the Marxist-Leninist doctrine. In June

1990, free elections were held in Bulgaria for the first time since 1939.

Eric had never seen his father so happy. He was so excited and full of new hope before the elections and so disappointed when the Bulgarian Socialist Party (BSP) won them again. He almost had a heart attack. They had to call a doctor to give him some medications and calm him down. These were the same people from the old Communist Party, which over just a few months had transformed miraculously into, as they said, a new modern socialist party.

The country's economy collapsed. The stores were empty. There was not enough food and not enough gas for the cars.

"I will not be alive to see the time when Bulgaria will be completely free of the communists. They have just changed their names and pretend to be different, but they are the same corrupt and cruel party. They are the same people who till yesterday were calling themselves communists. I do not trust them. For me it is too late, but you have to leave the country before they close the borders again. Go! Take your family to Canada, and help your nephew as well when he is ready to emigrate," Santo told his son, Eric, and his wife, Renee.

His father continued, "Eric, emigration is not for everybody. But I know you will go through it. I know you. Since you were a little boy, you have studied and worked hard. You did not waste time at parties. Your mind is set up differently. You are prepared for this. Emigration is not easy; be ready because it will be very difficult for both of you. No matter how hard it is, do not think of coming back! Come only after you become Canadians, and only to visit."

When Eric and Renee bought their tickets, the inflation had eaten up all their savings.

Just a year earlier, a ticket to Ottawa was 1,300 leva. When they bought their four tickets, each one cost 12,500 leva.

They used all their savings. They quickly sold their car and furniture, and still they lacked 6,000 leva. Eric remembered his parents gave him the money from the savings they had.

How could they have saved 6,000 leva with a salary of 200 leva? How many years had they worked and saved to be able to pay for half a ticket? Eric wondered. His eyes got red as he thought of his parents' sacrifices.

He almost physically felt the pain of their disappointments. So many lives, so many people had broken hopes. Maybe their kids would continue searching for a better life.

Eric remembered their first rented apartment in Ottawa. It was two weeks after they arrived.

Since they had been staying with Eric's uncle Avedis, it was their first night alone with four of them in this foreign country, Canada. The kids were sleeping.

Eric and Renee were watching television and trying to understand it. They couldn't grasp what the news reporter was talking about. Eric switched from English to French. It was the same. They looked at each other and held hands.

"I thought I understood English," Eric said with a crooked smile.

"But if you don't, how are you working?" Renee asked.

"Well, Dave helps me a lot. He speaks with me slowly and often repeats what he is saying so I can understand him well," Eric said.

"How do you understand the other employees in the factory?" Renee asked him.

"They all are emigrants. They all speak very basic English, so I know all the words and their sentences are very simple." Eric was now laughing.

"I need practice. I need to listen more to how the local people speak English. I have to watch more television as well," he said.

"I registered for an English course at a college. The classes will begin in a month, three times a week, starting at 6:30 p.m. and lasting till 10:00 p.m," Eric told Renee.

"How about studying French? We have to learn French as well. We are living in Ottawa, and here you have to be bilingual to find a good job," Renee said, with panic in her voice.

"We will learn both languages with time. I have to emphasize my English at the beginning, so I can properly do my job. You also know some basic English from the university in Bulgaria. You will start learning French first, though. This way we will cover both languages when we are together. Once I start doing well in English, I will begin courses in French after work. You will do the opposite," Eric said.

"How long do you think it will take to start understanding the news on the television?" Renee asked, still holding Eric's hand.

"I don't know. For me, I will need maybe six months or a year to understand the news in English, and at least two years for the news in French. It should be the same for you, but in the opposite order," Eric said.

"You are too optimistic, as usual. I think we will need at least two years for the first language and three for the second to be comfortable in both languages and just for understanding and listening to the TV. To start talking comfortably, it might take much more," Renee said.

"For the kids, it will be much easier. They are young, and they will pick up the two languages in a year maximum. They will soon start school. The emigration office is so well organized. They already registered the kids at school in special level for children of just arrived immigrants. They will first learn French since they studied it in Bulgaria, and then they will continue their normal education, including English," Eric said.

Seeking a Better Life

"Eric, I'm afraid for the kids. We do not know in this country what is good and what is not for them. We will not know who their friends are. We are now totally confused and unable to give them advice. How can we be good parents?" Renee was letting her feelings come out.

"Yes, I know. I feel the same way. The only thing to do is to stay close to them and to learn at the same time what they are learning. This will mostly be your task. Study what they study. Help them with the lessons. Then we will see. Also, my cousin, Dave, is like a brother to me. He will give us the right advice. I trust him," Eric said.

"You have to also learn how to drive a car, so when you start working one day, you'll be able to go by yourself. One day, we will have two cars, Renee, and we will both go to work," Eric said emphatically.

"What are you talking about? We have nothing right now—only two suitcases with clothes. How can we buy a car?" Renee said with a shaking voice.

Renee was panicking. "I will never be able to drive a car here. I'm so scared. Everything is so new for me. I do not know the rules. And who will hire me to work when I do not know how to speak?"

"Do not worry! Everything will be all right. Right now you have to take care of the kids and start learning French," Eric said.

"Let's try to sleep!" he added and turned off the TV.

The noise of the city was loud, and the apartment they had rented was just a basement with a big glass sliding door, which did not muffle the ambulance sirens.

It was scary, and both of them were listening and thinking the same thing.

Why are there so many ambulances passing by? Is it safe in this city? What's going on? The sirens never stopped and were driving them crazy.

"I will turn on the TV. Maybe we can sleep better with the TV on," Eric said.

Renee came close to him and slowly fell asleep.

Eric remembered his mother's advice when he was a boy:

"Eric, you have to prepare yourself in advance to be able to one day be successful. You have to study, and you have to get up early in the mornings."

Eric started planning what he needed to do to prepare in advance.

The first and most important thing is to find a good apartment in a good area of the city. It must be around good houses and close to a nice shopping center; it will inspire us when we belong to that part of the city.

Second, Renee has to register and start the French courses.

Third, I have to register and start learning the rules of driving, and then take the exam so I can have a Canadian driver's license. So far I'm driving with the international driver's license, which is good only for six months.

Fourth, I have to start intensively learning English in a college. I need to practice talking and writing. I have to start reading books in English as well.

Fifth, I have to register and take courses on Saturdays on the computer—Lotus and Word. Dave uses this software program Lotus 1-2-3 in everything he does. I have to be as good as he is so we can work better together.

Sixth, in about three months, I have to register to take beginner French classes. I have to be able to at least start understanding French. Some of the employees speak only French. To be their manager, I have to learn French as well.

Eric looked at the TV. It was 4:30 a.m. He got up carefully, so as not to awake his family. He did his ten minutes of gymnastics. He took a refreshing shower. He shaved his face, got dressed, and took the keys to the factory and the company car. He kissed his wife and the kids—all of whom were still sleeping—and left.

He had to be first at the factory. He would turn on all the lights and all the machines so when the employees came at six thirty to six forty-five, the noise of the working machines would put them in the right working mood. He needed to see in advance the work in progress on every machine and what each of the employees had done the previous day. When Dave came at 6:45 a.m., he would be ready to start the new day. The factory started at 7:00 a.m. sharp.

Eric drove down the street, and he noticed that on the corner, not far from their rented apartment, was a big hospital. An ambulance was coming out from the emergency entrance of the building. Eric smiled, finally understanding what was going on last night.

A new day was starting, and he was full of hope and energy. He looked at the beautiful houses on both sides of the streets, and he dreamed that one day they would have their own house. They were in Canada. His dream and his father's dream were coming true. He had brought his family to a country where the values of Western democracy were guaranteed by the constitution. This country had proven with its long traditions that it followed those values.

Eric and Renee were going to do whatever it took to provide a better life for their family.

They had big hopes …